PERFECT
PARTNERS

PERFECT PARTNERS

•

JOYCE MARLOW

AVALON BOOKS
THOMAS BOUREGY AND COMPANY, INC.
401 LAFAYETTE STREET
NEW YORK, NEW YORK 10003

PRINTED IN THE UNITED STATES OF AMERICA
ON ACID-FREE PAPER
BY HADDON CRAFTSMEN, SCRANTON, PENNSYLVANIA

PERFECT
PARTNERS

Chapter One

Sara scanned the files stacked on one corner of her desk, frowned, then jabbed the red button on the phone linking her to her fourth secretary this year— and it was only June. "Would you get the Harvard and Stanford Law School files right away, Sandy?" She glanced at her watch. "My Recruiting Committee meeting starts in fifteen minutes."

She straightened her tailored jacket before cradling a dozen files in one arm, accepting another two from her secretary, and walking toward the elevators that would take her up one floor to the forty-first. Davis & MacGregor was the most prestigious law firm in San Francisco and represented powerful, moneyed clients willing to pay four hundred dollars an hour for the most sought after legal advice in the city.

Sara Jackson managed the firm's attorney recruiting program, hiring students from the top ten law schools in the country to clerk during the summer.

The process reminded her of a merry-go-round, and the brass ring was a chance at a high-flying legal career. But the firm extracted a price—long hours, loyalty, and absolute commitment. She'd never seen anyone turn them down or even question the system.

When she rounded the corner, she saw Lorenzo Duran headed straight for her. Squaring her shoulders, she took a calming breath. She wasn't in the mood for one of their sparring matches. Not today. Every time she saw Lorenzo, she saw trouble, and today was no different. He was the most promising law student in the firm's summer program, but he was also the most difficult. Definitely a high-maintenance man.

As she walked on, Sara noticed a dozen secretaries swivel around in their chairs as Lorenzo strode down the hallway toward her. There was something about him that made every woman at the firm sit up a little straighter and smile a bit brighter. *That* was another problem.

He stopped a few feet in front of her and waited, his arms folded across his chest. His stance, and the proud tilt of his head, suggested a self-confidence that Sara knew was well earned. In any other man, his attitude would verge on arrogance. With Lorenzo, it seemed somehow appropriate.

"How's your afternoon, Sara?" he asked a little too solicitously, jet black eyes flashing.

"Busy." She thought he sounded awfully happy for an overworked law clerk after a long day, and when he gave her a look she could only describe as virtuous, she knew he was up to something.

"Too busy for a small favor?"

Holding the files closer to her chest, she shook her head. "Sorry. I'm due at a meeting in ten minutes."

He stretched one hand out in front of her. "I'm desperate, Sara. I've got a legal memorandum due ASAP, and my secretary thinks five o'clock is quitting time." He opened his other hand to reveal three microcassettes. "Can you use your influence to find somebody willing to work late?"

Unconsciously, her brow furrowed. The firm's star law clerk had a reputation for keeping secretaries overtime, but it was up to her to see he got the help he needed. She pursed her lips and gave him a hard look.

"Speaking for management, your work habits are commendable, but that isn't going to help you find a typist. You've already developed a reputation with both word processing and the typing pool."

"For wanting my work done on time?" he asked, clearly offended.

"No. For wanting it done after hours. Haven't we discussed getting your dictation done earlier in the day, so we can avoid the five o'clock crisis hour?"

He nodded. "We have. Several times. And if I were in control of my hours, there wouldn't be a crisis. But that's not the case. It's Thursday, and Parker wants the first draft tomorrow and the final Monday. Mexico's considering a new law on intellectual property rights, and our client doesn't want the bill passed. Since I'm the only Spanish-speaking law clerk, I'm the logical guy for the translation."

"I'm sure that's not the only reason Parker put you on the project," she reasoned. "He must be impressed with your work."

Lorenzo gently waved the cassettes in front of her. "Then you'll help me?"

She gave him an uncertain look. "I don't know. It sounds like you and some unsuspecting secretary are headed for a nightmare of a weekend."

"No doubt about that."

She pursed her lips, then glanced at the slim watch on her right wrist, a necessary accommodation since she was a lefty. "Drop by my office and have Sandy put the word out right away. She's got a list of typists looking for overtime pay."

She reached into her pocket, retrieved a handful of notes, and held them out. "Your phone messages— some from this morning. Since I'm in charge of the program, I get stuck holding the bag when you don't answer your page."

He remained silent, giving her an unreadable look, which simply confused her. Why wasn't he cooperating? She gave him a look designed to kill lesser men, then arched one brow. "Haven't you heard the paging system calling your name all afternoon?"

He moved closer to scan the sheets of paper she held in her hand. "I've been holed up in the library all day. That's the only place the paging system can't be heard, and the only place I can get any work done."

"I do understand." She handed him the messages, then glanced at her watch again. "I've got to go or my meeting will start without me." She took a few steps down the hall, then turned back. "Let me know which secretary helps you out. I like to know the team players."

"Will do. I'm stuck here till eight or nine. If your meeting runs that late, I'll spring for pizza."

"No thanks. I'm skipping dinner."

A smile played at his mouth. "Luigi's. Thick crust, everything on it, hold the anchovies."

She hesitated, biting down on her lower lip. Luigi's was her weak spot, and she knew what waited at home. Her refrigerator held two cartons of yogurt, cottage cheese, and some leftover Chinese food of questionable age. Licking her lips, she decided. "Thin crust on the pizza. I started a diet yesterday."

Lorenzo raked a hand through thick, black hair and laughed, his white teeth a stark contrast to his dusky complexion. "Sure, thin crust makes a difference, and you don't need to diet."

She gave him a searing look that spoke volumes.

"Hey, the lady wants thin crust, she's got it." He gave in easily. "And, under the guise of eating pizza, we'll hit the highlights of the Recruiting Committee meeting."

"You know better than that," Sara began in an official tone that quickly changed to a drawl with a hint of speculation. "The secrets of recruiting meetings aren't for the ears of the innocents being reeled in hook, line, and sinker." She pointed a finger at him. "Especially the biggest, brightest fish in the pond."

He shrugged. "Can't blame a guy for trying to get the inside track."

"Yes I can. Now, if you'll excuse me, I'm late."

Lorenzo gave her a mock-salute as she walked away. He'd only known Sara a month, but he was impressed. She was both beautiful and highly capable—a rare combination. He left his cassette tapes with Sandy, then continued on to the law library. He opened both heavy glass doors and stepped into a world that had been denied him until just a few short years ago.

It was a world of intellect, creativity, and solutions. All that was his now, and he basked in the feeling of satisfaction that came with his new surroundings.

The huge room was lined with mahogany shelves every four feet, each filled with richly bound law books, texts, and treatises. There were six long worktables with comfortable leather chairs and ten computer stations running along one wall. Four printers were stationed in a small glass-enclosed cubicle to prevent noise from distracting the lawyers and clerks using the library. The room was deserted, just as Lorenzo had expected. The office hummed twelve hours a day, but late nights were his domain. That was when Davis & MacGregor shut down and Lorenzo put in extra hours.

It wasn't that he needed a leg up on the competition. Heck, he already had three job offers. He was spending the summer here to add one more to his arsenal of choices, but he intended to go the extra mile to earn it.

He sprawled in a winged chair the color of expensive red wine, a dozen law books spread out in front of him. He slowly unwound his long legs from around the chair, yawned, and thought about how good eight hours' sleep would feel; he'd been getting by on five. He folded the cuffs of his white shirt up on his forearms and wrote out the first draft of a legal treatise on contract law.

When he finally checked his watch, it was seven-thirty. Leaving books and papers in a jumble on the wide mahogany table, he quickly made his way through the now quiet office, down the Hayworth Building elevator, and across the street to Luigi's.

Twenty minutes later, he was back. ''Pizza,'' he announced, dropping the white cardboard box on

Sara's desk, moving some files, and settling himself on one corner. Opening the lid, he tore out a wedge-shaped piece and handed it to her.

Wrinkling her nose at the smell of cheese and Italian spices, Sara let out a long, appreciative sigh and took the pie in both hands. "Thanks. I thought you'd forgotten."

He shook his head solemnly. "Not possible."

Taking a big bite, she ran her tongue over her lower lip, catching the strings of cheese and sucking them into her mouth. A minute later, she took another, bigger, bite.

He laughed. "You're amazing. You must not weigh more than a hundred and twenty, and you chow down like a truck driver."

"I'm lucky. It's in the genes."

He bit down on the thin, crisp dough, chewed, and swallowed. "So," he said, his tone suspiciously casual. "How was your meeting? Talk about any law clerks I know? As in which ones might be receiving job offers?"

She shook her head. "You don't seem like the kind of guy who likes hearing the word no, so why do you keep asking questions you know I won't answer?"

He gave an impatient shrug, balled up his napkin, and threw it in the wastebasket. "I'm curious about the process. You know the score from my point of view. I've had a long time to think about it, and this is what I want—high-profile clients, power, and money. Joining the firm can give me all that.''

She straightened to relieve the ache between her shoulders, her hand moving restlessly to her hair. ''You know, you may want to consider another firm. Davis & MacGregor isn't always easy—in fact, it's pretty rough.''

He regarded her quizzically a moment, then his face clouded. ''So was growing up in the worst neighborhood in Oakland. I got out, but my mother's still there and I want to give her something better.'' The line of his mouth tightened a fraction. ''That means joining the firm that pays top dollar for the best legal talent. This is the firm, and this year that legal talent is me.''

Sara knew a little of his background, the one that wasn't listed on his résumé, but she hadn't realized how fiercely it had affected him. One night when they were both working late, light conversation had turned serious, and he'd hinted at having grown up the hard way.

She stood, leaned forward, and put her hands flat on the desk. ''Why don't you tell me about it?''

His laugh was tough—cynical. ''You mean the deep, dark, intimate details?'' He shook his head. ''You don't want to know any more than I've already told you, Sara. It wasn't like in the movies. Bad boy makes good and bears no scars. My neighborhood was one big gang war, and it never stopped. The

Tough Bloods, the Menacers, the Blades. I joined when I was ten.''

She straightened, the color draining from her face. ''But why? You must have known that would only lead to trouble.''

He fanned an impatient hand in the air. ''You don't understand. Not joining was never an option. The gangs hung out around the school. You couldn't get in unless you *did* join. And if they decided you could go, they extracted a price. You either paid, or you dropped out.''

Lorenzo walked stiffly to the window, his back to her. He didn't often think of those early days, not now that he was so far from those dark, desolate back alleys. But the angry, desperate child he had been could come back to haunt him, as it had now, much too easily for him to completely forget. He stared out the window at the San Francisco skyline, a hollow, implacable look casting a harshness to his features. Lights scattered across the hazy skyline like pinpricks of flame, a reminder of each test by fire he'd won, and how many more he still had to conquer.

After a minute, he went on in a low tone. ''I knew I had to go to school. And I did what I had to do. I finished high school, then bummed around till I hit twenty-three. That's when I got serious.'' He turned away from the window and folded his arms across his chest. ''It took me six years to finish college, but I got my degree.''

Unconsciously, her brows drew together, forming a subtle vertical crease between them. "Six years is a long time for undergrad. How come?"

"My father skipped out about the time I started high school. I had two younger sisters. Mom's job barely covered the rent, and sometimes not that. She did piece work in a garment factory—still does, for that matter. I started working at fourteen to keep food on the table."

When her mouth dropped open, he shrugged. "Going home helped me in other ways. In college, I was intimidated by all the white faces. The only Latinos in college weren't from the barrios. I hardly ever spoke in class my first two years." A long, slow smile softened his features. "At home, I knew who I was."

Sara tried to understand how far he'd come, and at what price, but she couldn't. Lorenzo's expression gave nothing away, but she could sense there was a minefield behind his dark eyes. And somehow, she knew it wouldn't take much to set off an explosion. Finally, she said, almost in a whisper, "Your memories are so different from mine. I can't imagine being part of a gang, trying to—"

His mouth curved in a bitter half-smile. "Don't turn sentimental on me, Sara. It may sound like a James Dean movie, but it isn't romantic when it's real."

"I didn't mean . . ." she started, then stopped, realizing there was nothing she could say. "My childhood was so different, so ordinary, I can't imagine the things you talk about.''

With a long, exhausted sigh, Lorenzo slowly ran a hand over his face. ''Ordinary is good, Sara,'' he said, sounding very tired. ''Hell, it seems only yesterday I was that tough kid, wearing a rebel image like some tarnished shield. Like it was something to be proud of. I doubt anyone from the old neighborhood would even recognize me today.''

''Why's that?''

He flashed her a quick look she couldn't read.

''Trademark shaggy long hair tied with a bandanna, torn jeans . . .'' He shrugged impatiently. ''Black leather jacket. The usual tough-guy image. It may have been late in the game when I decided to play in the big leagues, but once the decision was made, I knew I had to adopt a corporate image.'' He glanced down at his tailored slacks, long-sleeved white shirt with black monogram on the cuffs, and burgundy striped tie. ''And that's what I've done. I can walk the walk—do whatever it takes.'' His voice took on a hard edge. ''It's what I want. And I'll play by their rules because I intend to win.''

Sara leaned against the wall, watching him carefully. She hadn't known him long, but she'd already figured out he fit the mold. He'd do well at Davis & MacGregor. He was ambitious, his ego was as big as Kentucky, and dollar signs danced in his eyes.

Just like her ex-husband. Three years of marriage

had convinced her there was a lot more to life than money. If she ever married again, it would be to a man who put his family first. And to be on the safe side, she had one hard-and-fast rule—she never dated lawyers. Their careers generally came first, with their families a distant second. Her father was the only exception she knew, and the chances of finding another man like him were pretty small. He was a successful corporate attorney, but he'd been her best friend ever since she was a little girl.

Running her tongue over her lower lip, she considered what had gone on in the Committee meeting she'd left an hour ago. The more she listened, the more she knew Lorenzo would fit in perfectly at Davis & MacGregor, and since the news would hit the streets tomorrow anyway, she wasn't really giving away any secrets. Just a twelve-hour inside edge.

She glanced at him with half-lidded eyes and chose her words carefully. "You know those rules you're following? The ones that'll make you a name at the firm?"

"Yeah."

"Well, they keep getting tougher every day."

Lorenzo blanched. "How's that?"

"The Recruiting Committee made some decisions tonight. They could have kept the news secret, of course, but the partners encourage competition between the law clerks, especially with the job market in a stranglehold. The word'll be out tomorrow through some *unknown* source.''

She hesitated, and his face clouded with uneasiness. She purposely kept her voice neutral when she went on. ''The firm's only making seven offers to this summer's class of law clerks.''

There was a moment of strained silence between them. Lorenzo closed it. ''And since there are twelve of us in the program, five clerks will walk out of here with no job after law school, right?''

Sara nodded again, watching the look that crossed his face. It was more pensive than angry. Anger was what she'd expected. Then, the truth was, she didn't know what to expect from Lorenzo. She watched his eyes turn smoky and his features soften, then even out. He had a way of hiding his emotions; she'd seen him do it before. Everything about him set him apart from the other law clerks—even his age. He was thirty-two and the others were in their twenties.

Lorenzo drew his lips in thoughtfully, then gave her a hard look. ''Jobs are tough to come by these days, even if you graduate from an Ivy League school. I already have offers, but I want this one. Something tells me I'd better get back to the library.''

She glanced at her watch; it was eight-thirty. ''You're on the right track. The firm approves of workaholics.''

''I'm just stacking the odds, Sara. And making sure they're in my favor. See you tomorrow.''

Watching him leave, she had to wonder at the hours he put in, and whether he'd still think the rewards were worth it in a few years. Her husband had, but his blind ambition had destroyed their marriage. After a minute, she glanced at the papers strewn over her desk, very much afraid she was getting caught up in the same game.

She had a dozen projects waiting for her at home and still hadn't started renovating her turn-of-the-century Victorian house. She'd felt adrift after the divorce, in need of a purpose, and she didn't seem to find it at work anymore. She'd looked forward to drawing up her own plans, even doing much of the work herself. So far, she hadn't had time to do anything other than dream.

Suddenly she realized she hadn't seen her parents in weeks. She picked up the phone and dialed their number but, after a dozen rings, slipped the receiver back in the cradle. They were probably out to dinner. She stared at the unfinished paperwork on her desk, then glanced at her briefcase. After a long pause, she retrieved her purse from under the desk and headed for the door.

She looked back once, turned off the lights, and left.

Sara got to the office early the next morning and was on her second cup of coffee when she heard the knock. Looking up over her reading glasses, she wondered where her secretary was, then saw from her watch that it was only eight-twenty. Office hours didn't officially start until nine, and Sandy usually showed up at five till.

"Come in," she called out, closing her notebook when Paul entered. She waved the Senior Partner to a chair. He was in charge of recruiting and technically her boss. She set her glasses on the desk. "What's up?"

Paul Robertson flicked an imaginary speck of lint from his very narrow Armani lapel. "A run-through on tomorrow's yachting soirée, for starters. We're expecting a premier showcase for both the firm and this year's class of law clerks. I just talked with a partner at Phillips, Matthew & Sutton. They're taking their clerks on a wine tasting excursion through Napa Valley, including hot air balloon rides." He gave Sara a deliberate look. "I'm sure what you've got planned will top that. I wouldn't want our clerks to feel slighted."

"They'll be impressed, Paul," she reassured him, remembering the long hours she'd put in planning the party.

"Good." He nodded slowly. "That's exactly what I want. Now give me a rundown."

She leaned back in her chair and ticked off the list she'd worked on for weeks. "We leave Pier 41 at three o'clock, although there's a half-hour leeway for latecomers."

Paul pursed his lips. "Good."

"Champagne, both California and French, will be served all afternoon, along with an open bar. Hot and cold hor d'oeuvres until five, dinner at seven."

"Did you get that new chef? The one Mac wanted?"

"It took some doing, but when the Mac in Davis & *Mac*Gregor asks for something . . . Yes, the master chef's on board."

"Excellent." Paul put his hands together, the fingers lightly touching each other. "What about music?"

"A jazz pianist. Plays weekends at The Mark."

Paul dipped his head slightly, and she went on.

"We'll spend a few hours sailing around the Bay, under the Golden Gate Bridge, to Sausalito and Tiburon, and head back around sunset."

"Excellent. Did you come in under budget?"

Sara replaced her glasses on the bridge of her nose and pulled out another notebook. She found the page she was looking for, then ran her finger down the columns. "Budget was seventeen thousand, I'm at sixteen-four. There will be some last-minute additions, but it's close."

Paul gave her an approving look and arched his brows. "Well done. This affair's costing a bundle, but we're known for doing things top notch. I hope the clerks will see the kind of life they'll have if they join the firm. We're particularly interested in Kramer and

Lockwood, but Duran's at the top of the list. He has several offers pending, but I'm sure he'll choose Davis & MacGregor.''

She removed her glasses and rubbed the bridge of her nose. ''That won't be easy. We'll have to beat the competition.''

Paul waved his hand dismissively. ''Of course. At sixty-five to start, we're already five thousand above our competition; I figure we'll throw in another five as a signing bonus.''

A soft gasp escaped her. ''I know he's tops in his class, but what's the big draw?''

''His work is excellent, he's articulate and impeccable, and I'm told the clients are quite impressed. If that weren't enough,'' he went on with a smile, ''he works twelve-hour days and appears to thrive on pressure. Under my guidance, I'm confident he'll bring new clients and significant revenue to the firm.''

''It sounds like you've got big plans for our star.''

''Absolutely. He's motivated by money, and if it suits our purposes, we'll accommodate him.'' Paul narrowed his eyes. ''Is he bringing a date tomorrow?''

''No, I don't think so.''

Paul stood. ''Good.'' He rocked back on his heels, then shot her a swift, searching look. ''I'd like you to spend some time with him, one-on-one. I want to know how he feels about the firm.''

''I can already answer that, Paul. He's impressed.''

"I expect him to be impressed," he said calmly. "What I want to know is if he's ready to consider an offer. He's been here a month, and we've only got another two weeks before he goes to that free legal clinic where he's finishing the summer. I want you to find out what's on his mind."

Paul started for the door, then turned back and gave her another searching look. "I don't care how you get the inside track, Sara. Just do it."

Chapter Two

That afternoon Sara found Lorenzo in the library, hunched over a stack of law books at a back table. His hair was disheveled and a thick lock darkened his forehead. He'd followed his usual habit of rolling up his shirtsleeves two turns, and his strong forearms were dusky against his stark white shirt. She leaned against the tall library shelves and watched him for a moment. He was engrossed in what he was writing on the blue-lined, yellow legal pad, occasionally glancing back at the law book that lay open in front of him. The aura of focus and purpose surrounding him almost shouted through the silence.

"How's it going?" she asked quietly.

He put his pencil down, leaned back in his chair, and stretched. "Other than being tired, it's going fine.

This brief is massive, and I've still got a long way to go." He glanced at his watch. "I can still put in a few hours, then hit it again tomorrow."

Sara guessed that he was more than tired; he was probably exhausted, but she also knew he had to attend the yacht party tomorrow. He'd already missed a couple of opportunities to socialize with the partners, and another no-show would be a big mistake. No matter how much the firm wanted him, they expected him to toe the line. There was an unspoken but unbreakable agreement at the firm—they paid top salaries, and everyone performed.

"You're working Saturday?" she asked.

He briefly closed his eyes. "I need to, but there's that yachting thing I'm expected to attend." He raised his brows. "Unless the Recruiting Administrator can get me off the hook."

She shook her head from side to side. "Not a chance. This is a command performance, with no way out."

He sighed. "Makes me wonder how much of this summer is about work and how much about fitting in with the big guys." "There *is* some truth to that," she agreed. "My first year at the firm I was amazed at how much time and money was spent on entertaining law clerks." She folded her arms across the front of her beige linen jacket. "Four years later and with a recruiting budget of three hundred thousand, I see it as one way Davis & MacGregor maintains its status as the top firm in San Francisco. We're adding clients instead of downsizing like most firms, so we must be doing something right.''

Lorenzo's dark eyes mirrored his frustration. ''Maybe so, but I thought what counted was how good a lawyer I'll be. When am I supposed to write this brief—in my sleep?''

''I know it must be difficult juggling—''

''I'm not complaining,'' he interrupted. ''I know Davis & MacGregor is the hottest game in town, and the social perks are part of the hiring strategy, but I want to concentrate my time where it counts.''

''And that's what you should do,'' she agreed. ''But a big part of that is getting to know the partners on a personal level. You can't do that when you spend all your time hitting the books.'' She opened her hands expansively. ''You have to go tomorrow.''

He frowned, a suggestion of annoyance in his eyes. ''I don't see why this yacht party is so important.''

She regarded him carefully. ''Then I'll tell you.''

Lorenzo grinned, leaning back in his chair. ''It's about time I wrangled some inside information out of you. Let me have it.'' His silky voice held a challenge.

Seeing the amusement in his eyes, she laughed and shook her finger at him. ''Keeping your nose to the grindstone is important, but don't lose sight of the other criteria for getting that offer.''

''Such as?''

"How well you interact with clients, and your flair for rainmaking."

"Which means—"

"Bringing in more clients and revenue to the firm."

He pursed his lips and nodded. "The light dawns."

"Exactly. And the partners won't get a feel for how charming you can be, or how persuasive, if you spend every waking moment in the library."

He gave her a wide-eyed, imploring look. "Do I do that?"

She rolled her eyes. "Tomorrow. Be there."

Breathing in the sharp scent of the harbor, Sara felt the slight trace of salt air on her skin. As she walked slowly across the gray, weathered planks of Pier 41, she angled her hand in front of her forehead and squinted into the dazzling sunlight.

The magnificent yacht that stretched before her for what seemed a city mile strained against the foot-thick, coiled rope that held it fast. The long hull glistened pristine white against the water, and the azure sail covers positioned along the deck were a brilliant match for the blue, cloudless sky. The yacht looked more like a photo in a slick travel magazine than the real thing.

She walked up the gangplank, greeted the Captain, then made her way topside. Reaching the brass railing running the length of the hull, her eyes widened. The party scene rivaled a glitzy, sun-dazzled movie-of-the-week on prime-time TV. She'd planned the party in every detail, and it already wore the elegant look of success. Scanning the decks, she saw the expected number of attorneys and spouses or current significant others, and a few heavy-hitting clients. The party was a thinly disguised invitation only, no excuses allowed, combination business and recruiting function.

''Champagne?''

''Thank you,'' she told the man in a starched white uniform holding a silver tray of delicate crystal flutes. She took a sip and glanced around the deck, noting the gleam of polished teak, shining brass fittings, and bright green-and-white striped lounge chairs placed in small groupings. The staff all wore impeccable uniforms and hovered at the edge of the party. She also noticed the tables were spotless, with no glasses, napkins, or soiled plates in sight.

The invitations had specified casual wear, and the men wore creased twill trousers or tailored knee-length shorts, monogrammed polo shirts, and the obligatory deck shoes. The women wore a kaleidoscope of brightly colored sundresses, although she did spot a few younger women in white linen shorts and sleeveless silk T-shirts. Sara had chosen a bright pink sundress in a pattern of polished swirls that skimmed low on her thighs and left her arms and neck bare.

Reminding herself that it was part of her job to mingle, she joined a group of the younger wives.

They were all noticeably blond, with contact lens– blue eyes and incredibly tanned, tautly exercised bod- ies. She walked into a conversation about tennis pros, which turned to health spas that took ten pounds off in a week, and on to whichever charity thing each wife was doing this season. Sara found an excuse to leave, then headed for the stairwell. Feeling a hand at her elbow, she turned around and almost collided with a set of shoulders that were incredibly wide, bare, and molded bronze. Lorenzo gripped her forearm, steady- ing her.

"Whoa! Did you arrive on a whirlwind?" He smiled, his dark eyes hinting at mischief.

Sara took a deep, calming breath. "You could say that. How's the party going?"

He shrugged and answered offhandedly. "As par- ties go, I'd say it's good."

"Only good? I was hoping for better than that."

"Well, I don't—"

Both turned at the sound of her name being called. It was Paul.

"Everything appears in order, Sara," Paul told her. "This should be the start of a very successful day." He extended his hand to Lorenzo. "Good to see you."

"Wouldn't have missed it. Sara's certainly put to- gether an impressive party."

Paul shrugged matter-of-factly. "That's her job."

Sara drew back, wondering if Paul was in one of

his moods or if there were something more to what he'd said. Paul liked keeping people off guard.

"Sara . . ." Paul started. "If you've got a moment?"

"Of course." She turned to Lorenzo. "I'll catch up later."

"I'm counting on it," Lorenzo said in a low voice, watching Paul steer her toward the round teak bar at the rear of the yacht where MacGregor waited. The yacht picked up speed, causing the wind to whip across the deck. He slanted a half-lidded glance at Sara as her dress blew around long, tanned legs. She was beautiful, and he'd wanted to spend more time with her. He couldn't help but think she was walking in the wrong direction—away from him.

Around five o'clock, Sara combed her hair for the last time, looked down at her pale blue two-piece bathing suit, and wished she'd brought something else. The suit she'd thought perfect for sunning at the beach suddenly seemed skimpy. At least she'd remembered to bring along her cover-up, even if it was only a few inches longer than the suit. Leaving her things in the cabin set aside as a women's dressing room, she quickly climbed the stairs. When she reached the deck, Lorenzo, Kingsley Kramer, and two other law clerks were standing at the railing. Lorenzo caught her eye, smiled, and waved her over. Remembering her instructions from Paul, she joined them by the ship's railing.

"We were reminiscing about the law school grind," Lorenzo told her when she reached them.

"Comparing notes between Harvard and Stanford?" She glanced from Lorenzo to King.

Before King had a chance to answer, Anne Lockwood, a short blonde who was as competitive as the men, interrupted. "And Northwestern."

"I'd never forget my alma mater," Sara said, brushing wind-whipped strands of hair out of her eyes.

"You're from the Midwest?" Anne sounded surprised.

"No. I was raised in San Jose, but Northwestern has a good Economics program, so that's where I went."

King leaned back slightly, a smug look on his face. "Stanford always ranks either first or second in the country."

"That's certainly true for the law school," Sara agreed, ignoring his tone. Not for the first time, she thought King was a little too full of himself. She turned toward Anne. "Are you enjoying the party?"

A delighted grin spread over Anne's face, all the way up to her eyes. "It's wonderful. Never thought I'd spend the afternoon on a yacht. We don't have anything like this at home. And the music is very nice." She glanced at the ebony baby grand positioned on the deck. The pianist wore a staid black tuxedo, but his hair was slicked back in a trendy ponytail.

"I'm glad you like it," Sara said.

"I do, except . . . do you think anyone would mind if we asked for some, uhm, younger music?"

Sara laughed. "Ask away. It's your party."

Anne elbowed King in the ribs. "How about jazz?"

"Or some new-age," he suggested hopefully. "See you all later. We've got an afternoon to liven up."

Sara slid a glance past Lorenzo and out over the water. The waves were getting choppy, and the yacht slipped heavily through the iridescent blue water. She found the back-and-forth rhythm soothing; it reminded her of a well-used rocking chair. For a moment, she leaned against the railing and let her shoulders drop. It had been a long day; it was only half-over, and she was tired. Scanning the skyline of San Francisco, she remembered she was here to work. She was supposed to ask Lorenzo some questions, and it didn't matter that she was tired, or that she didn't much like doing it. It was her job. And if she wanted to convince Paul to get her that assistant, she needed to deliver.

Taking a big breath, she started. "The summer program is so hectic, the time slips away before you know it. I checked my calendar, and you've only got two weeks left at the firm."

He nodded. "That seems about right."

"I understand you'll be working the rest of the summer at a legal clinic for the poor."

Lorenzo pulled a green-and-white striped chair next to where she stood so he could straddle it and fold his arms on the back. "I'm headed for an immigration clinic in downtown Oakland."

"Really? Seems like an odd place to want to work." When he gave her a puzzled look, she stammered, "I mean, compared to Davis & MacGregor."

"I'm looking forward to the change," he said simply.

She looked out at the choppy waves and frowned, wondering if he was purposely being vague. Surely he didn't think he needed to add to his reputation as the strong, silent type. She cleared her throat. "I'm surprised. I thought you were ready to hop on board the Davis & MacGregor bandwagon."

"I am, but this is a chance to help people who really need it. The clients are mainly Hispanic, and most don't speak English. They need help dealing with the paperwork so they can stay in the U.S. It's a lot different from working on a million-dollar, multinational deal."

"But I thought you wanted life in the fast lane— money, power, the all-American dream." Her eyes narrowed speculatively. "What changed?"

He opened his arms wide. "Nothing. I still want it all. But this job is a payback for my minority grants and scholarships. It's only right that I do something

in return. The clinic's a few blocks from my apartment, and I see people line up at five in the morning
waiting to get in, needing some help. They don't get
many law clerks because it's a volunteer operation.''

''No pay?''

''You got it. The only way I can afford it is because
Davis & MacGregor is paying me twice what I expected to earn this summer. Six weeks on the gravy
train, five in the bread line. It evens out.''

She hesitated, measuring him for a moment. The
more she got to know Lorenzo, the more she respected him. He'd given his career, and his life, a lot
of thought. She chose her words carefully, trying to
keep her tone noncommittal. ''If you stayed at the
firm all summer, you could bank quite a nest egg.''

''And leave the clinic high and dry?'' He shook his
head. ''Not my style.''

She nodded. ''So it isn't actually the work that interests you, you just want to put something back into
the community?''

''It's both.''

''And you're still interested in a job with the
firm?''

He threw his head back and laughed. ''You know
it.''

''And you're happy with the work we're giving
you?''

He moved next to where she stood by the railing.

"What's with the Dick Tracy routine? You knew I planned to work for another firm this summer."

She hesitated. "The Recruiting Committee always wants to know where we stand. And, if an offer is made, whether it will be accepted."

He leaned back to study her face, wondering at her questions and the reasons behind them. He'd hoped there might be more to them than a professional interest—maybe personal—but he was probably wrong. He'd noticed more than one of the firm's lawyers studying her perfectly oval face and big green eyes, but he'd never seen her return their hopeful glances. As far as he knew, she was all work and no play—strictly business. It was a trait they shared.

Sara glanced toward the back of the ship and saw one of the newer law clerks standing alone by the railing. She looked lost, or maybe she just didn't have anyone to talk to. "I'd better get back to my job," she said. "Catch you later."

Lorenzo stood and watched Sara's dark brown curls bounce against her shoulders as she walked toward the young woman. "I'd like that," he whispered under his breath. He noticed Robert Simms and Ken Thornton sitting together, apparently sharing jokes. He considered joining them. At least they could commiserate over the loss of a day's work. Although the partners were enjoying their little sailing soirée, it meant the clerks would be pulling ten-hour days; he'd push the wall to fourteen.

But first he had to get through today, and that meant being sociable with the socialites. Squaring his shoulders, he turned away from his friends and thoughts about Sara and walked decisively toward the attorneys standing around the bar.

It had been a tough week. Sara had filled Paul in on Lorenzo's plans, even though she'd felt slightly guilty. Then they'd talked about a project Kingsley Kramer was working on. Finally, she'd brought up the idea of hiring an assistant. Although Paul hadn't said no, he had put her off until next week. When she'd been married, it had suited her to work as many hours as her husband; he'd been almost as ambitious about her own job as his. But since the divorce, she'd discovered she wanted more than just a career. Having taken the first step, she was anxious for the second, and even a few hours a week would make a difference.

As she turned the corner, she saw Paul coming toward her. Judging from the heavy briefcase he carried, he was probably through for the day. Most partners took work home, and Paul was no exception. He stopped a few feet from her. "Glad I caught you. Saved me from calling you at home tonight."

"What's up?"

"MacGregor's going to Mexico for one of his entertainment clients and wants Lorenzo along to see how he deals with the big boys."

"I'm guessing you want me to make travel arrangements?"

Paul gave her a searching look. "More than that. How's your passport?"

She frowned. "It's up-to-date. But—"

Mac's gruff voice stopped her as he joined them. "Good. You're both here." He turned to Paul. "Find Lorenzo Duran. I'd like to see him before I leave."

"Right away." Paul bit out the words, then walked swiftly down the hall.

Mac turned to Sara. "I take it you heard about the Cancún trip."

"Yes."

"I want to leave first thing Wednesday, and I want you along."

Sara briefly closed her eyes, feeling suddenly tired.

"It's another urgent matter for Shadow Star Films," Mac told her. "I'll need your administrative skills for whatever comes up. I want two other clerks along—the best we've got. Check with your Committee partners and give my secretary their personnel files—and Duran's."

Sara nodded. "I'll meet with the Committee first thing in the morning." She took in a long breath, realizing her dream of working fewer hours was just that for the foreseeable future. She'd been on working trips with Mac before and knew it meant an exhausting work schedule.

"This trip will give me an opportunity to see if I

agree with the majority of the Recruiting Committee,'' Mac said. ''They all think Duran is our top choice.''

Looking past his shoulder, Sara saw Lorenzo striding down the hallway. ''Lorenzo's headed this way,'' she said, keeping her voice low.

Mac turned. ''Good; this saves me looking you up.''

''Yes sir, Mr. MacGregor.''

Mac frowned. ''I appreciate the measure of respect, Duran, but I'd prefer you call me Mac.''

Lorenzo paled. ''Yes, si—, uh, Mac,'' he stammered, disbelieving that he was on a first-name basis with the head of the firm.

''Good. That's settled. I have an important business deal and you're in. It's a contract dispute, which may not sound too exciting, but in this case the players make it both difficult and very interesting.

''Why's that?'' Lorenzo asked.

Mac slid his hands in his trouser pockets and rocked back on his heels. ''The entertainment industry is always difficult. You're dealing with inflated egos, and there's a tremendous leverage in a money game this size. Shadow Star Films is my biggest client. I negotiated the contracts for their last movie, and the producer, Aaron Brooks, insists I handle this little *problem* that's developed.''

Curious about Mac's cynical tone, Lorenzo waited patiently. This was his chance. He'd be in on an international deal, working with the name partner, the man with the power. "I have the evening free," he offered. "If you have time to sketch out the problem in more detail, I can start the groundwork tonight."

Mac folded his arms across his chest. "I like your style, Duran. If you're going to be on my team, it's smart to ask questions. Even smarter to find the answers. But the name of this problem is Conchita Domingo."

Sara frowned. "Didn't she star in one of Aaron's films last year?"

"Yes. Her contract calls for a personal trainer, hairdresser, makeup artist, cases of her favorite bottled water, and dinner hand-fed to her cats at lunchtime."

Lorenzo frowned. "And the producer hired her again?"

"Absolutely!" Mac answered immediately, punching the air with his fist. "That movie made Brooks the hottest producer in Mexico and a few million bucks. For that, you put up with difficult."

"I see your point."

"The problem is, now she wants to renegotiate her contract halfway through the shoot. Highly irregular, of course, and, according to the terms of her contract, impossible. But Mexico's reigning answer to Madonna doesn't play by the rules. Aaron's willing to give her what she wants"—He gestured sharply with his right index finger—"to a point. It's up to me to negotiate that point closer to the producer's side than Conchita's.''

Pursing his lips, Mac absently ran a hand through his thinning hair. ''Sara, check with my secretary in the morning. We need a full set of contracts, both Spanish and English. Better bring a laptop computer as carry-on luggage. We'll be working during the flight.''

She nodded. ''Should I book seats in first class?''

''Absolutely. There's no way I can work in coach. Lorenzo, your main job will be to translate. Conchita doesn't speak English.'' He shot him a curious look. ''You should also know that she's overly fond of handsome young men. Watch yourself, or you'll be on the front page of the tabloids.''

Lorenzo forced a smile. ''Yes sir, but if the tabloids are to be believed, Conchita's hot-tempered and impetuous. I hear she goes through men as often as she colors her hair.''

Mac leaned back his head and laughed, then slapped Lorenzo on the back. ''You're right there, son.''

Son? Lorenzo swallowed hard and noticed Sara staring open-mouthed.

''Of course, you can always ask Sara to run interference,'' Mac told him with a wink. ''I often bring her along to troubleshoot and handle whatever details come up.'' He glanced sharply at Sara, assessing her with narrowed eyes. ''I trust Sara implicitly.''

Sara cleared her throat awkwardly. "Is there anything else? I've got a lot of work to do."

Mac waved his hand. "That'll do for now, but check with me in the morning."

Glancing sideways, Lorenzo caught Sara's expression before she turned and marched down the hall. She didn't seem too happy about something. "How long do you think we'll be gone?"

"Four, maybe five days."

That meant they'd return to San Francisco about the time he left the firm to work for the immigration clinic. When he'd made his plans, it had seemed perfect. Work the first half of the summer making big bucks and the second half learning immigration law.

Suddenly he wasn't so sure. He was going to miss Sara.

Chapter Three

After the long flight to Cancún, they'd gotten a good night's sleep, and the next morning they headed out to the movie set ten dusty miles from town. After meeting the director and watching a scene being filmed, they'd gone to the trailer Aaron Brooks utilized as an office. That had been at two o'clock. It was almost six. Four hours of negotiations, and they still didn't have a signed contract.

Mac paced three feet in either direction while dictating still another revision to the producer's secretary. Her fingers moved quickly over the keyboard of her computer, then she hit the print key and handed copies to Mac, Aaron Brooks, Conchita Domingo, and Lorenzo. Kingsley had been the only other law clerk chosen for the trip, but he was occupied with reworking some other documents for Mac.

Sara fanned her face, deciding it must be eighty degrees in the trailer and close to a hundred outside. Her raw silk dress and pantyhose were stifling. She envied the men, who had gotten down to rolled-up shirtsleeves hours ago. She'd been surprised when Lorenzo had been the first to unfasten the top two buttons of his shirt, yank off his tie, and drape it across Brooks's desk. He'd repeatedly run a hand through his hair, which was disheveled, and his close shave ten hours ago now looked like a shadow across his square jaw.

It didn't seem to matter what he did, or what he wore; Lorenzo acted as a magnet for female admirers. Conchita had almost salivated when she'd first seen him, batting her eyelids until the mascara had flaked off her lashes, leaving a rash of tiny black dots. It crossed Sara's mind that she should let Conchita know that she was wearing a cute pair of raccoon eyes. It would have been one of those "woman-to-woman" courtesies. But, after watching her flirt with Lorenzo for the better part of an hour, she'd decided not to bother. Crossing her legs, Sara sighed as Conchita tossed her long jet black mane over one shapely bare shoulder and turned toward Lorenzo.

"¿Tiene luz?" Holding a slim cigarette between fingers that flashed long, red-lacquered nails, Con-

chita brought it to her lips. Glancing at Lorenzo through thick black lashes, she waited impatiently. A bored, pouty expression softened her features.

He withdrew a sleek gold lighter from his front pocket, purposefully flicked it open, and touched the flame to her cigarette.

Conchita gave him a boldly suggestive look, then sucked in air until the end glowed red. *"Gracias,"* she purred before glancing back to the contract. Pointing one slender finger to page four, she asked, *"¿Qué quiere decir esto?"*

Lorenzo arched his brow at Mac, then explained in Spanish. "That's the clause you requested. The clothing allowance for"—he slanted his eyes at the tall, blond hunk standing off to one side, burly arms crossed over his chest—"your masseur."

"Ah, *Sí.*" A satisfied smile tugged at Conchita's mouth. Yawning behind one manicured hand, she dropped the contract on the table, abruptly pushed her chair away, and stood up. *"Estoy cansada. Es todo para hoy."*

At Mac's glance, Lorenzo said in a low voice, "She's tired. Wants to make it a day."

"Aaron will change her mind. There's no reason we can't wind this up tonight."

Lorenzo sat back, exchanged looks with Kingsley, and watched. Brooks was well respected in the entertainment industry and one of Mac's biggest clients.

Maybe he'd learn something about strategy, or about difficult women.

As Brooks tried to convince Conchita to approve the latest revisions, Lorenzo found it increasingly difficult not to laugh. The more Brooks cajoled, the harder she resisted. When she set her lips in an impassioned pout, and shook her hair so furiously it whipped around like a whirling dervish, he knew she wouldn't budge. And when Brooks immediately backed down, he realized just how much power the actress wielded.

He bent closer to Mac. "No dice. The filming of the *corrida* is tomorrow, and she's due on the set at eight."

"*Corrida?*"

"Bullfight. It's an important scene and she'll want to prepare."

Mac nodded. "Her role's the female matador. Aaron can't argue with that. Besides"—he shrugged— "Conchita would be mad as hell if she woke up with smudges under her eyes." He pursed his lips thoughtfully. "The ones she's got now are bad enough. We probably won't get much done tomorrow, but I'd like you all on the set. Production shuts down periodically all day, and I'd like you available."

After Conchita flounced out with her entourage, they made their way toward the limo. Glancing at King, Mac said, "I've got an early morning meeting with Aaron tomorrow. I'd like you to be there."

Kingsley brightened. "Sure thing, Mr. Mac-Gregor."

"And I'll send the limo back for you around ten," he told Lorenzo and Sara.

"Fine," Sara whispered, relieved at the thought of sleeping in.

Mac shot a quick look at Lorenzo. "When did you take up smoking?"

Lorenzo glanced sideways at the older man as they walked along. "I didn't."

Mac's brows shot up. "You just happened to have a lighter in your pocket when Conchita needed one?"

"I managed to dig up a few newspaper photos of Conchita." Lorenzo's tone was carefully nonchalant. "She always seemed to be smoking, so I thought a lighter might come in handy."

Mac's mouth twisted wryly, but he stopped short of a smile. "Nice touch, son." He clapped Lorenzo on the back. "When you get here tomorrow, look for the action. Once filming starts, that's where I'll be, and I want you close by."

Sara silently chalked up one more point for Lorenzo. When he wanted something, he obviously went all out. She knew Mac was impressed. She silently counted the miles back to the hotel, reckoned it would take half an hour, and decided she couldn't wait that long. She'd been doing her best not to think about the grumbling noise coming from her stomach, but she couldn't wait any longer. "Mac?"

"Yeah?"

"On our way to the hotel, could we stop at one of those little stands and get a dozen tacos?"

His face was expressionless, then he shook his head and grinned. "You and that appetite."

She gave him a hard look. "I'm so hungry I'd eat a cow if somebody'd cook it."

Mac didn't answer, but smiled wearily as they climbed into the limo. After they were on their way, he reached for the white telephone that was part of the conference equipment. "We'll go over the contract again over dinner. I intend to come up with something to *dazzle* Conchita." He punched a series of numbers on the keypad, then put the receiver to his ear.

"Yes, this is MacGregor. Casita number three. I'd like room service for four delivered in about an hour. Do you still do that spicy prawn dish? Good. And steak and chicken fajitas with all the trimmings?"

Putting his hand over the receiver, he asked, "Anything else?"

"A beer would be great," King said. "Two even better." He leaned back against the leather upholstery and cocked one leg over the other knee.

Mac looked at Lorenzo and Sara. "How about you?"

Lorenzo shook his head.

"Iced tea," Sara suggested.

"One beer, three iced teas," Mac said into the phone.

Sara knew King had made a mistake. They'd probably work for two or three hours, and Mac didn't hold with drinking on the job. This was a time to impress the boss, not relax. One strike against King, and she knew he had only two left.

Her mind on the rumbling in her stomach, she glanced hopefully at Mac when he hung up the phone. When he stared back blankly, she darted her tongue over her lower lip. "But we're stopping for tacos first, right? I mean, I could starve waiting for those fajitas."

Three hours later, Mac stood up, wearily stretching his arms. "Let's call it a night. I'm set for my meeting tomorrow."

Sara flipped the screen of the laptop computer closed, slipped her eyeglasses into a leather case and set them on the table. "You won't get an argument from me. It's been a long day."

Lorenzo stood. "You coming, King?"

"I'll be along in a minute." He nodded almost imperceptibly. "You two go ahead."

Lorenzo looked from King to Mac, then walked across the room and opened the door, waiting for Sara.

"See you in the morning," she said in a tired voice, then headed through the doorway and into the tropical Mexican night. The sky was a shade somewhere between indigo and midnight black, the moon a slivered crescent. The hotel consisted of a two-story, red-tiled building facing the ocean, with dozens of small adobe casitas nestled on each side. Wide stone pathways connected the casitas with a huge, iridescent swimming pool. The moonlight shone on the water's surface, highlighting the little ripples with pale, iridescent gold.

Sara's heels tapped into the silence. "At least we don't have far to walk. These shoes are a killer."

Lorenzo stopped, holding out one hand, palm up. "What?"

"The shoes, Sara. You're done for the day."

Smiling, she held on to his arm, then scissored each leg, removing the offending shoes and handing them over. "Thanks."

"No problem," he murmured, hooking a finger under each heel and carrying them in one hand.

"Do you think Conchita will sign the contract tomorrow?" Sara asked. "We didn't give her everything she wanted, but we came close."

Lorenzo let out a tired breath. "Let's put a cap on business for the night. Okay?"

Sara nodded.

"Right now, I'm thinking more about a swim. Want to join me?"

"It is warm. And these hose feel like wet, clammy socks." Sara ran one hand through her disheveled hair, brushing it away from her face and taking in a long, ragged breath. "A swim does sound good."

He stole a look at her, recognizing the look of exhaustion shadowing her features. She was tough. She hadn't complained once, even though the day had stretched to twelve hours. "I'm not interested in laps," he said gently. "Lazy lounging is more what I have in mind."

She let out another long breath. "Wonderful."

They were walking along the far edge of the pool, where stands of lacy, waist-high ferns clumped together. The long fronds almost hid the passageway running between two pool cabanas, and there wasn't much light. Lorenzo noticed Sara kept glancing down at the pathway, careful to watch where she stepped. It was as if she didn't realize he was there to catch her. To stop her from stumbling. He reached out and cupped her elbow in his hand, gently steering her along the path, easing her closer to him.

When he saw a puzzled look on her face, it occurred to him that she didn't know he felt responsible for her. In his world, a woman took that for granted. In hers, he supposed a man didn't necessarily want to take care of a woman. For Lorenzo, that was as much a part of him as breathing. They reached the entrance to Sara's casita and stopped. He held out one hand and opened it palm up.

Sara blinked several times.

"Your key, Sara. Give me your key so I can open the door."

"I can open it myself," she stammered, fumbling in her purse.

He set her shoes on the ground and tried to take the key out of her hand, but she held on tight. He let out an exasperated breath.

"I don't see—"

He threw his hands in the air, then ran them raggedly through his hair. "Because in my culture, when a man walks a woman home, he sees that she's safely inside before he leaves. Do you mind?"

Her mouth dropped open. She clamped it shut and handed him the key. The thought that he was being courteous hadn't crossed her mind. Suddenly, she realized she was letting old dragons haunt her. Would those demons ever retreat into the distance, along with the past?

Lorenzo opened the door with a flourish, relieved she'd finally acceded. "I'll change and meet you at the pool."

"In about ten minutes," she told him as he left the circle of light. Inside, she realized with a start that there was a lot about Lorenzo that she didn't know. Along with some things about herself that she'd forgotten. Like how it felt to be with a strong man—and to be cared for. It felt curious, and very comforting.

She glanced around the room, admiring the high ceilings of the casita, and the white, roughly textured

adobe. The room was large and airy, awash in red and
gold flowers in clay pots. A dozen handcrafted baskets were artfully arranged on a dully shining Mexican tile floor. Sara picked up one of the baskets and
ran her fingertips over the intricate pattern of the
reeds. As a child, she'd spent countless afternoons in
her mother's fiber arts studio watching her weave.

She remembered being fascinated by the twists of
brightly colored hand-spun wool her mother wove
into specialty blankets and wall hangings. She'd spent
hours learning how to plait long, graceful reeds into
light, airy baskets, then reproduced dozens of tradi-
tional patterns—mostly Native American. Finally,
she'd had the confidence to begin designing her own.

The French doors leading to the terrace were open,
sheer opaque curtains billowing back into the room
like a cloud of fog. The image reminded her of San
Francisco, and she had a wave of homesickness. Just
then, she heard a knock at the door. She turned and
took a deep breath. It had to be Lorenzo. But hadn't
they agreed to meet at the pool? She hadn't even
started to change. She glanced in the cut glass mirror
that hung on the wall, ran a hand through her hair,
then moved with certainty toward the door. She
reached out her left hand, held her breath, and turned
the brass doorknob.

As the door swung open, the light from inside the
casita threw a pale glow across the tiled entryway
where Lorenzo stood waiting. He was no longer wear-

ing the tailored gray trousers and white dress shirt he'd had on ten minutes ago. Instead, he wore black swimming trunks, a white towel around his neck, and a recalcitrant smile.

"I was already back to my casita when I realized I'd left these on your doorstep." He held out both hands, offering a red high-heeled shoe in each.

She took the shoes. "Thanks." She lifted her chin and met his gaze. His eyes were dark and unreadable, but she sensed tension in the lines of concentration along his brows. The sensation traveled the distance between them until it felt like a rubber band stretched tight.

He reached up and grabbed each end of the towel draped around his neck. "Want me to wait for you?"

"Sure. I'll just be a minute." She walked into the bedroom, pulled off her clothes, and tossed them on the bed. She rummaged in her drawer for her suit, wondering why everything seemed so difficult between them, why nothing came easy. She slipped into her blue two-piece, grabbed a towel, and headed for the door.

They walked quietly through the night, then came to the black wrought iron gate leading to the pool. Lorenzo held the door open and she strode inside. She tossed her towel on a low-slung patio chair, kicked her sandals off, and walked to the edge of the pool. She didn't hesitate, but dove headfirst into the opalescent water.

When she'd finished five laps, the tension she felt had subsided, though she still wasn't clear on its origin. She only knew that Lorenzo had a maddening effect on her, and she reacted before she had time to think. And she couldn't see any good reason for that. She came up out of the water at the deep end to find him sitting on the edge watching her, his long legs dangling in water that glimmered with moonlight. She shook the water from her hair, glanced at him, and, just as quickly, glanced away. No matter how she wanted to feel, he still made her nervous.

"Had enough?" A slight, teasing grin touched the edges of his mouth.

She ran one hand over her face, blinking away the chlorinated water that made her eyes sting. She reached up and grabbed onto the ladder leading out of the pool. "What do you mean? I thought you wanted to swim."

"I did. But it seemed as if you were racing somebody or something. Which was it?" Gliding into the water beside her, he balanced himself by holding onto the ladder with one hand. A questioning look remained on his face, then he smiled very faintly, still staring down at her until she finally looked away.

"Are you angry with me?" he asked gently.

She glanced back. "Angry? No, but you *are* stubborn and mule headed, and you do insist on having your way."

"Just because I wanted to open your door for you? Wanted to make sure you were safe?"

She pursed her lips and thought a minute about what he'd said. Maybe she'd been wrong; maybe she was remembering her husband. With him, everything had been like a war.

"If that's what it was, I'm sorry." She gave him a searching look. "It felt more like a control issue."

He didn't respond; instead, he threw back his head and laughed.

"What's so funny?"

"That you'd even think that!"

Her foot found the bottom rung submerged in the water and she climbed out, embarrassed and oddly angry. She stood looking down at him, her body dripping with water, her skin sleek and wet. "Okay. You made your point. Maybe I was wrong."

For a moment he stared back, then his glance softened. "Don't be mad at me, Sara. That's the last thing I want."

Her heart jolted, then calmed. She had the sudden desire to get away; it was almost as if she were being pulled in a direction she didn't want to go. Grabbing the towel from where she'd tossed it on the patio chair, she ran it quickly over her face and arms.

Lorenzo pulled himself out of the pool and reached for his towel.

She slipped into her sandals. "It's late. I think I'll turn in."

He looked at her, but she avoided meeting his glance. "I'll walk you home."

"No, thanks. You still haven't had your swim."

"But I—"

"I'm fine. Really." She glanced at him then, trying not to notice the wounded expression on his face. She didn't want to hurt his feelings, but she couldn't stay another minute. Retreat seemed the easiest solution.

"Good night," she called over her shoulder as she strode through the gate and made her way toward her casita. Walking quickly down the path, she decided to climb into bed and shower in the morning. Right now, she didn't want to have time to think about anything. Especially how she felt about Lorenzo.

Sara glanced at her watch again, then wiped away the sweat that beaded at her temples and trickled slowly down her neck. The morning had passed quickly and it was after three. She'd pulled her hair back, tying the strands with a ribbon of yellow silk and dressing for the heat in a full-skirted white cotton dress. But the low scooped neck made her wish she'd brought a hat and sunscreen.

Being on location in Cancún had its high points, but twelve-hour days in the stunning heat wasn't one of them. The scorching hundred-degree heat had parched her throat and burned her bare arms and neck an uncomfortable shade of pink.

They'd been filming the opening procession of the

corrida all day, but there had been problems—mainly
with Conchita. She'd kept the crew waiting more than
once, missed her lines, then acted petulant and quarrelsome when Brooks ordered retakes. It seemed as if
she were purposely holding up production, and the
unsigned contract was a likely reason. Brooks finally
lost his patience around two and halted production to
resume the negotiations. Since Mac hadn't needed her
at the meeting, Sara had spent the last hour wandering
around the picturesque plaza de toros.

She'd found the colorful pageantry fascinating.
Though she knew the reality of a bullfight would be
appalling, she could understand how people were
mesmerized by the suspense and danger. In Mexico,
the much loved running of the bulls was not a simple
choice of life and death for the animals. It was an
opportunity for them to die heroically, with thousands
of spectators cheering the fearlessness of both the
graceful matador and the raging bull.

The three-level spectator gallery only held five hundred people, small for bullfights but perfect for filming. She stood a short distance away from the film
crew, watching men dressed as picadors and bande-
rilleros saunter by in exquisitely embroidered costumes. Hundreds of colorfully dressed peasants
wearing broad-brimmed sombreros and wide straw
hats had taken their positions in the three-tiered arena.
Filming was about to start.

The band began to play and the *alguaciles,* or constables, dressed in ornate sixteenth-century costumes from the reign of Spain's Philip the Second, strode onto the blistering, golden sand of the arena. The constables and the local *presidente* went through the elaborate ceremony of turning over the key that opened the gate to let in the bulls, then kettledrums rumbled and trumpets blared. An expectant hush ran through the crowd and the *toril* gate was thrown open. A huge black bull exploded into the ring and galloped savagely around the empty circle, stopping to lower his great head and hook his horns tentatively into the heavy board fence circling the arena. The crowd roared.

Sara was leaning with her elbows on the top of a section of that fencing when Lorenzo came up beside her.

"A magnificent *miura,* that one," he commented over the noise, leaning into the wall a scant foot away from her.

She glanced sideways. *"Miura?"*

"Bulls of death." He lifted his face into the sun, then turned toward her. "Spaniards have bred fighting bulls for centuries, but this breed"—he nodded toward the massive bull trotting back and forth in the ring—"has killed more men than any other."

Sara stared at the bull, her eyes wide in both fascination and repulsion. "I can't imagine how the matadors get over their fear, knowing they could be gored or killed."

"To fight a bull when you are not scared is nothing; and to not fight a bull when you're scared is nothing," Lorenzo rationalized calmly. "But to fight a bull when you are scared"—his voice rose in indisputable reverence—"now *that* is something."

She gave him a curious look, wondering why he knew how it felt to face fear. She felt certain it had something to do with the hand he'd been dealt as a child, and although she wanted to ask, she didn't. That would be stepping over the line separating their personal lives from the office. She didn't know how Lorenzo felt about it, but she wasn't sure she wanted to cross that line.

She noticed King walking toward them. When he was within a few feet of them, he gave Lorenzo a sly, calculating look. "You missed the fireworks, pal."

"I've been watching the film crew."

King made a clicking sound with his tongue and gave Lorenzo an apologetic look, although he sounded anything but. "Wish I could have joined you, but Mac wanted me there for the negotiations."

Sara smiled inwardly at his self-important tone, thinking that at least he was consistent. Maybe his attitude had something to do with his name.

"Did I miss anything?" King asked.

Lorenzo glanced over his shoulder to see Mac headed their way. "Conchita will be on in a minute. I'm curious to see if she works the cape herself."

King stared out at the huge bull and shook his head. "No way, man. If she's smart, she'll use a double."

"How'd the meeting go?" Sara asked Mac as he joined them.

"The contract's signed."

Her eyes widened. "How did you manage to turn that around? I thought Conchita had her heels dug in."

Kingsley gave a short, derisive laugh. "It was something, I'll tell you that. The lady's an amazing piece of work," he bellowed, then waved his hand dismissively. "But Mac handled her like a lion tamer with a pretty little she-cub."

Sara frowned, then glanced around to see if anyone close by had overheard. She knew Mac didn't hold with discussing clients or their problems in public, and certainly not in King's mocking tone.

Mac had a grim expression painted on his face, and she waited expectantly for him to say something. He didn't. He just folded his arms across his chest and stared intently at the arena. For a minute, she wondered what he was doing, then realized he'd given King a long length of rope and was waiting to see what he'd do with it.

By her count, King was winding up for strike two, with only one chance at bat remaining.

She wasn't surprised when he fielded the ball to Lorenzo instead.

King took a step back and shoved his hands in his

pockets. "Wasn't that about the way you saw it, pal?"

Lorenzo tipped his face to the sun, then looked past King and made eye contact with Mac. "It's true that Aaron gave in to most of her demands. But there was more to it than that. Aaron knew what he was doing. When a director's been shooting and reshooting one scene all day, and the female lead can't get it right, you're faced with two choices." He shrugged. "Cut your losses or go for broke."

King shook his head. "I don't get it. Conchita held the cards in this game."

Mac's expression gave nothing away as he turned to Lorenzo. "Is that how you saw it?"

Lorenzo shrugged again. "Aaron had two possible plays—give in to Conchita's demands, or replace Mexico's hottest, most bankable star halfway through the film."

"But he did give in," King insisted.

"You could look at it that way," Lorenzo agreed amiably. "But what he got in return was a finished movie. He didn't have to reshoot most of the scenes, and he saved both time and money." He arched one brow. "Probably millions."

Sara made the connection and grinned wryly. "I get it. Four hours and six takes might have been Conchita's way of making a point, right?"

"Exactly," Mac interjected. "A procession of the

bull, and the matador and picadors entering the arena, does not require six takes.''

''Tell me if I'm wrong,'' Lorenzo said hesitantly, ''but it's my guess Conchita paid quite a price for that contract, and she may get a lot more than she bargained for.''

King was clearly puzzled. ''But the contract didn't cost her a whit, and she got almost everything she wanted.'' He opened his arms wide. ''She won.''

Lorenzo shook his head. ''Ms. Domingo may be a good actress, but she hasn't learned much about business or long-range planning. Or the importance of Aaron Brooks and Shadow Star Films. Mr. Brooks did what needed to be done to get production back on schedule. He has stockholders to answer to, and that means watching the bottom line. Every hour production's down affects profit.''

Mac folded his arms across his chest. ''I'd say that's a pretty good summary. You missed some finer points, but—''

The crowd suddenly roared, and their attention was drawn toward the arena. They watched Conchita strut onto the pale sand, her pink silk and heavy gold lamé suit-of-lights an exquisitely sharp contrast to the blue-black bull pacing the other side of the arena. The picadors and their horses formed a line between Conchita and the bull, their eight-foot lances gleaming in the white-bright sun. After the film crew took shots of Conchita bowing to the crowd and gracefully sweeping her matador's cape from side to side, a slightly built young man strode into the ring and took her place.

Lorenzo pursed his lips. "Too bad. If she'd done the initial capework herself, the shots could have been much tighter."

King glowered. "Since when have you been an expert?"

Mac intentionally turned his back on King and swung around to face Lorenzo. "Have you considered the precedent for renegotiating the contract? If word gets out, and it will, the next star will want the same. What effect will that have on—"

King put both hands up, gesturing widely. "Since we'll be handling the negotiations, it means a lot more revenue for the firm."

Sara grimaced. King had tried to capitalize on the discussion instead of contributing anything important, or showing significant interest in the real issues. They all knew why Lorenzo and King were in Cancún— so Mac could decide who would get offers to join the firm. Lorenzo had proven himself at every turn, but King apparently didn't realize he was way off base.

Mac slanted his eyes. "You missed the point about long-term planning, King. Shadow Star Films has been my client for over ten years. Fees for a few contracts are a short-term issue. We're more interested in helping structure the client's business in a positive way. That means long-range planning for the firm, too.''

Noise erupted from the arena, and they watched as the picadors moved aside. The bull began pawing the sand with its front hoof. The matador waited, his red cape poised. A thousand pounds of black fury charged its human target, and the matador flashed the cape dramatically. The audience roared. The matador completed a graceful turn, then sauntered a few feet to one side, brazenly ignoring the retreating bull. The noise in the stands was deafening.

Lorenzo slid his hands in the pockets of his twill trousers and rocked back on his heels. ''Mr. Brooks showcased a very talented and beautiful actress in one of his films last year,'' he said, raising his voice above the crowd. ''As I recall, she was nominated for an award for her supporting role in *Desert Sunrise*.'' He looked directly at Mac. ''Is Sofia Martines currently under contract?''

Sara glanced at Lorenzo, impressed. She knew he didn't have a particular interest in the film industry, but he'd apparently learned a lot about Shadow Star Films. How else would he know who had acted in one of Aaron's pictures last year?

Mac didn't answer right away. Instead, he studied the arena for a full minute, then glanced over to where Conchita waited under a shaded, striped awning with a dozen people hovering around her. He shook his head several times, then leaned back and smiled.

"No, son, we don't have Martines under contract, but you've hit on an excellent idea. How'd you like to work on that project when we return to San Francisco?"

"Very much, but I'm afraid I can't."

"Can't—" Mac started, but Sara interrupted.

"Lorenzo's finishing the summer in Oakland, clerking at an immigration clinic."

Mac blew out a big breath, then ran a finger around the loosened collar of his white dress shirt. "I'd forgotten about that. Turning to King, he said, "How about finding Aaron's secretary and tracking down a signed copy of the contract." He glanced at his Rolex. "We'll meet you at the limo in half an hour."

King started to open his mouth but must have thought better of it. "Yes sir," he said and walked away. He looked back over his shoulder once, but kept on walking.

Chapter Four

Mac nodded imperceptibly to Sara, and she stayed where she was. He waited until King was out of earshot, then leaned toward Sara. "The Recruiting Committee isn't going to like what I'm going to do, and I'm counting on you to explain for me. I'll be out of the office all next week."

She was caught off guard, but managed to answer. "Of course."

When Mac turned to face Lorenzo, Sara did the same. His eyes were sharp and assessing, and although he seemed to be waiting patiently for Mac to go on, she guessed he was coiled tight as a spring. She was pretty sure she knew what was coming, but Lorenzo didn't. He was about to climb a giant step on that ladder of success he had so firmly pictured in his mind.

Mac stepped away from the fence separating them from the arena, his profile sharp and commanding. He stood silently for a moment, studying Lorenzo with a calculating look. ''Aaron Brooks echoed my thoughts earlier today when he said he expected to see you at the firm next year. Having the confidence of a major client helps me cut through a lot of formality and go with my gut instinct. I've been watching you,'' Mac went on, a smile flickering at his mouth. ''You're intelligent, but more important, you're shrewd. And life's taught you about patience, fighting for what you want, and staying in for the long haul. I know all about your past and the obstacles you've overcome.''

Lorenzo started to interrupt, but Mac silenced him with his hand.

''That experience, and your maturity, gives you a unique insight into situations that most lawyers at the firm don't have''—Mac paused for a heartbeat and shook his head—''and, I dare say, never will.''

Sara watched Mac carefully. He was a firm believer in timing and presentation, and he couldn't have set this up better if he'd had a script. The oppressive heat of the day, the life and death struggle between bull and matador, the heady atmosphere of the movie set— it made for a compelling scene. She wondered if Lorenzo was as taken by all of it as she was.

"You're going to be a good lawyer, and I don't want to come up against you in the courtroom," Mac told him. "You're a winner, and I want you on our team. I'm making you a formal offer to join the firm."

Lorenzo swallowed hard and tried to act calm. He didn't feel calm. He felt disoriented. This wasn't the way it was supposed to happen. He was supposed to get a phone call, then a confirming letter on heavy, embossed stationery with a watermark you could read right through the parchment. An offer to join the best law firm in San Francisco was supposed to be planned, serious, and very professional. Instead, a major achievement in his life was being played out on a blistering hot movie set in Mexico.

"You're making me an offer now?" He fought to keep his voice calm.

"Yes. And because this is slightly unusual, I'd like your answer now."

Lorenzo took a deep, measured breath, trying to sort out what was happening, and why. He knew he should be ecstatic, but instead he felt pressured. He glanced at Sara, surprised to see her jade green eyes widen. She hadn't known Mac was going to make him the offer now. Why?

"And," Mac went on, "we'd like you to remain at the firm through the summer and while you're preparing to take the bar exam. Of course, you'll be on the payroll while you're studying; we won't expect you at the office. There is a deal coming up in Mergers and Acquisitions that I'd like you to work on.'' His eyes narrowed. ''What do you say?''

Lorenzo swallowed hard, wondering what benefit there was to accepting now. He also wondered how the Recruiting Committee would feel about having their power usurped. If the firm wanted him now, they'd want him when they made their other offers. If he accepted now, would he be making enemies? All other considerations aside, the issue of working at the clinic made his decision for him.

He took a deep breath. ''Of course, I'm honored—''

''You should be,'' Mac interrupted. ''We don't make many offers on the fly.''

Lorenzo took a deep breath. ''But I'm afraid I'm not prepared to accept right now.'' He regarded Mac carefully. ''And I'm committed to working the rest of the summer at the immigration clinic. I won't go back on my word.''

A shadow of annoyance flashed across Mac's face, then he tilted his head back and appraised Lorenzo calmly. ''I suppose we can wait. A month—no more.''

Lorenzo bowed slightly and extended his hand to Mac. ''Agreed.''

The men shook hands, then Mac turned to Sara. ''Tell the Committee I've made the offer, and that I expect them to come up with whatever terms it takes to close the deal.''

She nodded sharply.

Mac turned back to Lorenzo, who had paled at Mac's instructions to Sara.

"It's good to have a capable, articulate woman on your side to take the heat every now and then," Mac said. "Sara's a crackerjack and even tries to keep me in line when she gets the chance." He glanced knowingly at Sara. "But I think she'll agree with me on this one. How about it?" He opened his arms in question. "Does Lorenzo get your vote?"

She hesitated only a moment, but it was telling evidence of her uneasiness. Lorenzo wondered if her reaction was one of surprise at the unexpected offer, or indicative of a more personal concern about his joining the firm.

"Yes," Sara answered with deceptive calm. "He's got my vote. I'll meet with the Committee as soon as we get back."

Sara sat cross-legged on the floor of her mother's studio, a partially completed basket the color of dry summer wheat nestled between her legs. Her mother sat nearby, working the treadle loom her father had built from pine, oak, and maple woods. Her mother looked a good ten years younger than fifty-five, although she'd cheerfully admit her age to anyone having the temerity to ask.

"I'd forgotten how much I missed basket weaving," Sara said, twisting a long, pliant reed around the spokes that formed the framework for the willow field basket. Her gaze was drawn to the strands of milky quartz wool being drawn up into the loom where her mother worked. "The rug's going to be beautiful. What accent colors are you using?"

"Sea-foam green, indigo, and teal." Her mother expertly passed the shuttle from one side of the loom to the other, where she'd tied over a hundred strands of hand-spun wool.

Sara chose another long willow reed from the dozens soaking in a tall bucket, folded it in half, then looped the fold around one of the four sets of spokes. Sighing, she flexed her fingers a few times, then glanced up at her mother. "I'm out of practice."

Her mother slanted a questioning look at her. "Are you ever going to cut back your hours at work? The gallery's received several inquiries about your baskets and they're having a showing next month. Do you have time to finish a few pieces?"

"I couldn't commit to anything right now. Work has me pushed to the wall, but I've got my fingers crossed that I can hire an assistant soon."

Her mother nodded sharply. "Good. You need time for something besides work. The Navaho reproductions you showed a few years ago were very popular, and the market hasn't slowed a bit. In fact, it's booming."

"Handicrafts do seem to be 'in,'" Sara agreed. "Especially anything using natural dyes." She deftly wove the long willow reed around the base of the basket, then added thoughtfully, "But using dyes would be difficult right now."

"Why?"

"When I experimented with walnut hulls, my fingers were stained for days."

Her mother frowned. "Since when have you been worried about staining your fingers? You've been up to your elbows in color since you were a child."

Sara arched one brow. "My image at work. My career's important too, and it's hard juggling both."

Her mother thinned her mouth into a tight line. "I'd think Davis & MacGregor's image would be enhanced by having a professional artist on their staff."

A warm feeling enveloped Sara at her mother's words, but being a professional artist wasn't in her future. It was more of a dream. She remembered her first showing at Mary Dodd's, the small, elegant gallery in San Francisco. When the dealer quickly sold her baskets and requested more, she'd thought her career was launched. But problems with her marriage, then the divorce, had taken all her attention. Now that she was focused on her job there wasn't much time for anything else.

"Why don't you talk to your dad?" her mother suggested. "Maybe he can give you some pointers on how to juggle your life a little better."

"Good idea." Sara put the basket aside and stood

up. "It'll give me a chance for a closer look at that cabinet he's been sanding all morning."

A warm smile brightened her mother's face. "It was the one thing your father wanted from the auction last week, and he got it for a song."

"I know that made him happy," Sara said with a laugh. "See you later." She angled around the loom that took up nearly half the floor space in the light-drenched studio and went outside, through the back-yard, toward the old, detached garage her father had converted into a woodshop.

He'd been made partner at his San Jose law firm while she was still in high school, and they'd spent the next year under construction, adding her mother's studio, a three-car garage, and a swimming pool. Her mother's artistic skills extended to gardening, and no matter what the season, the yard was alive with color and scent. She breathed in the fragrance of rose and lilac bushes, then passed raised beds of colorful pe-tunias, geraniums, and begonias. Terra-cotta pots of impatiens and pansies splashed rings of crimson, pink, and purple on the redwood deck that shimmied around the kidney-shaped pool.

She eased the heavy garage door open and peered inside. As she inhaled the smell of wood and oils, memories flooded over her. Summertime, hanging out with her dad, watching him hand-cut his favorite dovetail hinges out of fragrant pine, listening to the whir of his table saw. She noticed an assortment of tools scattered along the battered workbench, projects in various stages of completion, and her father hunkered down beside a cabinet at the far end of the room.

"Come look," he ordered cheerfully when he saw her. "I'm about to paint and need your artistic eye."

The amusement in his voice didn't escape her as she threaded her way through the shop. "It's a great piece, Pop." She eyed the freshly sanded chest. It had a feeling of substance, stood almost waist-high, and held three big drawers. "Where are you going to put it when you're finished?"

He beamed up at her. "Your mother's studio. It's just right to hold all that wool she's got lying around."

"The drawers are nice and deep. What color are you painting the wood?"

He stood, almost a foot taller than Sara. His well-worn slacks and shirt hung loosely on his lanky frame. He took a step back and opened his arms in appeal. "Do me and your mother a favor," he suggested finally. "You decide."

She scanned the chest critically, then smiled comfortably to herself. "The studio's small. How about a creamy ivory, so the cabinet blends right into the walls."

He gave her a skeptical look. "Is creamy ivory sort of off-white?"

She smiled. "That'll do it."

He reached among a dozen paint cans until he found the right one. "The brushes are over there." He nodded toward the cluttered workbench.

Sara chose two, handing one to her dad and dipping the other in the gallon can. She moved the brush over the wood, careful to spread the paint evenly.

"Pop, can I ask you something?"

"Sure. What's up?"

She bit down on her lower lip and placed her paintbrush across the top of the open can. She'd always been able to talk to him. He was solid and dependable and laid things on the line. He hadn't coddled and protected her, and she'd been grateful for that.

"I love my job, Pop. I enjoy the travel, and the summer clerks are so enthusiastic about the law and the future. It keeps the job fresh and new."

Her father leaned back and gave her a sharp, assessing look. "So what's the problem?"

She ran a hand through her hair, then crossed her arms. "I don't know. There doesn't seem to be time left over for anything else. And I want to do more than just work."

He glanced down at her. "You know, you're part of your own problem, sweetheart."

Her mouth dropped. "Me?" She frowned and shook her head. "Think again. Paul's the one who piles on the work when I'm struggling to keep up with a dozen other projects."

"You have to learn to say no. Paul Robertson will

respect you if you put up boundaries. And if you don't, as Managing Partner of Recruiting, he has every right to assume you've agreed to his.'' He pointed his paintbrush in her direction. ''It's your job to convince him otherwise.''

Sara's lips twisted in a cynical smile as she realized he was right. ''Okay,'' she admitted. ''I see your point. I need to be more assertive.'' She walked over to the workbench, picked up a piece of wood, put it down, then absently examined another. ''Strength is an important trait in a man,'' she commented, turning the piece of wood over in her hands. ''Don't you think?''

He slid a puzzled look at her. ''Of course.''

''And courage.'' She met his eyes, then looked back at the wood she held. ''I mean, if I were describing a man I admired, those traits would be important.'' She blew out a big breath, knowing she sounded ridiculous and wishing now she'd kept her thoughts to herself. Glancing at the blank look on her father's face, she realized he probably wondered what had gotten into her. The problem was, she didn't know.

Holding up the piece of wood, she examined it closely. ''Is this cherry?''

''Yes,'' he said, the furrow along his brow deepening. ''Are you talking about Paul?''

Her mouth dropped open, then she threw back her head and laughed. ''God, no! I'm not sure I even *like*

Paul. I was just speaking . . . generally.'' Awkwardly, she cleared her throat and looked away, hoping to hide the flush that stained her cheeks. ''It has been a long time since the divorce, and I was just trying to put into words what kind of man I'd be interested in.'' She picked up several paintbrushes and needlessly moved them to the corner of the bench, then stacked them neatly. ''If I were looking, I mean.''

Her father stared at her a moment, then a slight smile tugged at the corner of his mouth. He picked up his brush, dipped it in the paint, and slowly stroked it across the wood. ''Intelligence is right up there, too,'' he said with enthusiasm. ''And it's important to be able to laugh. Life brings you problems enough without taking every little thing too seriously.''

''Uh-huh. That's for sure.'' Sara looked up quickly from beneath her dark lashes.

''If you were thinking of getting involved with someone, those would be important qualities to look for,'' her father said, glancing at her suspiciously. ''But, of course, you aren't . . . looking.''

Sara vehemently shook her head and gave him a wide-eyed, innocent look. ''No. No, I'm not.''

He nodded and went back to his painting, a satisfied look settling over his face. ''No, I didn't think so.''

''It's everything I've been working for,'' Lorenzo told his mother as she sat watching him pace back and forth over the threadbare carpet in her modest living room. Maria Duran had often likened her son to a stick of dynamite on the verge of explosion, and today was no different. Although he'd been a difficult child, she'd always known once he found the self-control to channel his boundless energy, nothing would stand in his way.

Maria edged back on the sofa and smoothed the hem of her cotton print dress. Smiling shyly to herself, she waited eagerly for her son's news.

"Davis & MacGregor has it all," he boasted. "Plush offices, state-of-the-art computer technology, and an impressive library. There's even a health club on the forty-first floor so I can work out whenever I want."

Maria listened open-mouthed. "It sounds like something on television."

Lorenzo's face broke into a smile. "I guess it does sound like TV, but it's better than that, *mamá*. I'm working with the best lawyers in the city. Most of the partners have national reputations, and two are in state politics. They make decisions that affect everyone in California." An expression of unabashed longing stole across his face.

Maria recognized that look and knew its genesis. Lorenzo had spent his youth courting the wrong side of the law, but his rebellion had transformed into ambition. She knew having a Harvard law degree would give him the same opportunities as sons born to wealthy men like the ones at this firm he talked about so much.

Lorenzo stopped at the end of the room and turned around to face her, fierce determination etched on his face. "Davis & MacGregor is synonymous with prestige and power. And that means money and everything that comes with it."

Maria sucked in her round cheeks, pursing her lips in disapproval. Her son's preoccupation with money concerned her. She thought there were more important things than how many pesos a man had in his pocket. "This firm, the one like a paperback book with trips to Cancún and movie stars . . ." Her voice trailed off, unamused. "Is this what they call 'life in the fast lane?'"

Lorenzo narrowed his eyes. "Funny, that's just what Sara called it."

"Sara?"

"She's the firm's Recruiting Administrator. I don't know what I'd have done without her this summer."

Maria noticed the slight flush that crossed his face. "Is this Sara your boss?"

His flush turned deeper and he angled his hands wide, palms up. "No, but she showed me the ropes and taught me how to work with secretaries, which attorneys to avoid, which ones have big cases, and clients who can afford to make new law—"

"You help make new laws, my son?" his mother

asked quietly, folding her hands in her lap. "How do you do that?"

"By having clients on the cutting edge of technology. The firm has the best. When problems develop between multimillion-dollar corporations, they can be costly, but most can't afford long, complicated trials. That's what you have to do to make changes in the law."

Maria nodded slowly, then smoothed her dark hair away from her face. She wondered at her son's familiarity with things so foreign to her. "So the companies that don't have so much money . . . they must accept things as they are and cannot make new law?"

Lorenzo paced down her tiny living room and back. "Yes, yes," he mumbled, but she wasn't sure he'd heard her question. He came to a stop and ran a hand over his chin. "I wish Mac had mentioned a starting salary, but maybe I can ask Sara."

"Your Sara must be in this 'fast lane' to know such things."

He chuckled, a slight grin softening his features. "No doubt about that. Her father's an attorney, so she grew up in the business and knows it inside and out." He folded his arms across his chest. "She's sure got Mac's ear."

"Mac?"

"Mr. MacGregor. He started the firm twenty years ago."

Maria shook her head. "I know these career

women are as ambitious as men, but I don't understand how a woman could have such influence. How old is your Sara?''

''Old?''

''Yes, how old, and how pretty?''

Lorenzo's mouth slanted upwards. ''She's a few years younger than me, *mamá* and, yes, she's very pretty.''

Maria frowned and clicked her tongue against her teeth knowingly. ''This is also like television.''

Lorenzo stood looking over at her, a bemused expression on his face. Suddenly he reached down and pulled her off the couch and into his arms, where she barely reached his chest. He hugged her quickly, then stepped back.

''Life is good, *mamá*. There's nothing for you to worry about. I'm taking care of everything and soon, very soon, all our problems will be over.''

Maria gasped, her heart pounding and her throat suddenly dry. An almost forgotten fear knotted inside her. ''What problems? Are you in trouble?'' she asked tremulously, her voice breaking.

''No, I'm not in trouble.'' He laughed and gave her a reassuring smile. ''You don't ever have to worry about that again.''

She sighed heavily. ''I know, my son. But sometimes I have memories.''

''Forget them,'' he demanded sternly. ''I have.'' He grew restless and resumed pacing. ''I know I

could have ended up on the wrong side of the law.''
He glowered. ''Most of the homeboys I went to
school with did. But I can't change the past. I can
only live in the present and build a future that is right
for me.''

He stabbed his chest with an index finger, then
glanced slowly around the small living room. ''I want
to get you away from here. I want you to live in a
nice place.'' He opened his arms wide. ''Have all new
furniture.''

Maria lifted her chin in the air. She'd raised her
children here in this blistering neighborhood of rundown apartments and small, cluttered houses with too
many children crowding the rooms. She'd lived in
dread of seeing her son come home with a knife or
bullet wound, but she'd managed to keep them together, to keep them a family.

''This is my home,'' she said proudly. ''And yours
too.''

''I know that, *mamá*. But wouldn't you like to live
in a nice house instead of an apartment? Some place
bigger?''

Maria looked around her, trying to judge her home
with the critical eye of her son. She saw the worn,
gold tweed carpeting with tracks a shade lighter leading through the doorways, but remembered the happy
sound of children running through the rooms. She saw
the secondhand couch, but remembered sitting quietly
in the evenings, her children held tight in her arms.

She looked again and saw the bright yellow and sea green curtains and slipcovers her eldest daughter had helped her sew last summer, and the cream-colored walls she's spent all week painting just a few months ago.

She frowned, sad to realize her son only saw poverty where she recognized wealth. "I'm happy here," she said abruptly. "And I don't need a big house. My daughters are married with children, and my son works very hard; he has little time to visit."

Lorenzo sighed loudly and ran his hands through his hair. "You're right, *mamá*. I haven't spent much time with you this summer. I promise I'll try and find time—"

She wagged her finger at him. "Spend your time finding a wife and give me grandchildren!"

"There's plenty of time for that," he insisted.

Maria looked away, saddened by his quick dismissal of her deepest wish—more grandchildren. "What about your Sara? Is she a nice girl?"

"She isn't *my* Sara, and yes, she is nice." He gave her a teasing smile. "She's single, too . . . well, divorced, but that's practically the same thing."

Maria pressed her lips together, but managed a wan smile. Suddenly she was very much afraid a problem had crept into her life. Her son rarely mentioned any woman by name, but he'd talked about Sara several times. It was past time for Lorenzo to find a nice girl who wanted to get married and raise a family. Sara sounded like she was more interested in a career than babies. Maria wanted Lorenzo to be happy, but she feared he was headed for heartache.

She reached out and gently touched his arm. ''Be careful. Don't let your heart lead you down a path you cannot walk. You make yourself fit into this other world, but you are still my son.''

Lorenzo's dark eyebrows slanted in a frown, then he drew his lips in thoughtfully. ''You worry too much, *mamá*. I know exactly what I'm doing.''

Chapter Five

Monday had proved to be exhausting, and Sara still had two meetings to attend. She was ten minutes late for the Recruiting Committee meeting when she walked through the doors of the conference room. The conversation stopped, and a dozen heads turned toward her. All were male except one.

Patricia Clayton was the lone female attorney on the committee. Tiny, she was a good head shorter than most of the men, with a cap of sandy brown hair and a small face without a trace of makeup. But there was nothing doll-like about her. There was a lethal calmness in her steel blue eyes, and she wielded power as effectively as Paul. His two-year stint as Managing Partner of the committee was up in a few months and

Pat had made it clear she wanted the position. So had Richard Goldman. Sara's money was on Pat.

"Good afternoon." Sara scanned the room quickly, then walked to the one empty chair at the conference table and stood behind it. Her emerald green linen suit splashed color in a room filled with steel gray, stark black, and stolid brown. Only Pat Clayton warmed the room with mauve silk.

"Sorry for the short notice," Sara apologized. "Mac's out of town, and he asked me to hold this meeting in his absence.

"What's up?" Paul asked sharply, his expression strained. "Our regular meeting isn't for another week."

Sara could tell he felt outgunned by the unexpected summons, but that couldn't be helped. Mac called meetings of both the Executive and Recruiting Committees whenever he wanted. She'd called Paul earlier to brief him on the situation, but his secretary had insisted he was too busy to talk. Maybe next time he'd be more amenable. She slid into her chair and placed one slim file on the conference table. "We have only one matter to discuss, and it couldn't wait that long."

Paul drummed the top of the conference table with the end of his pencil for a moment, seemingly annoyed, then set the pencil down and pursed his lips into a thin line.

Sara clasped her hands on the mahogany table in front of her. "As you know, Lorenzo Duran was on assignment with Mac in Cancún. Quite frankly . . .'' She let her voice trail off with a hint of expectancy. ''Mac was impressed.'' She glanced pointedly at the folder she'd brought with her. ''Of course''—she waved one hand nonchalantly, intentionally building the suspense—''his record at Harvard is stellar, including *Law Review*.'' She hesitated as long as she dared, knowing every eye in the room was focused on her. ''While we were in Cancún,'' she went on, ''Mac made him an offer to join the firm.''

She saw Paul's head shoot up, followed by several more, and struggled to contain the smile that tugged at the corners of her mouth. ''Mac is confident the committee will agree that Lorenzo will be a valuable addition to the firm.''

''Absolutely,'' Pat confirmed, her voice adamant. ''He researched several appellate decisions on summary judgment that went a long way in winning my motion before Judge Browning last week.''

Sara pursed her lips, glancing at the slight nods of several of the attorneys. It was obvious Pat's word counted a lot. She hesitated a moment, then went on. ''Mac couldn't wait for the committee's vote because time was a critical factor. Obviously, he wants your consensus, but sending Lorenzo off with an offer gives us a decided advantage.''

''I'm not sure I agree with that strategy,'' Paul commented dryly. ''Now Duran knows how much we want him.''

Richard Goldman laughed loudly, his good-natured attitude a sharp contrast to Paul's. "He knew that from the get-go. Besides, he already has several offers. He expected one from us, too."

Pat sat back in her chair and narrowed her eyes slightly. "We all agree Lorenzo is a hot commodity. My only question is, how do we get him to accept? Wherever he finishes the summer has an edge. Is he staying in the city?"

"Yes." Sara made a slight gesture with her left hand. "But in this case, advantage is hard to gauge. He's working for an immigration clinic in Oakland that serves clients below the poverty line."

Paul frowned. "Surely Mac asked him to stay the rest of the summer."

Sara nodded. "The clinic's a personal interest. Lorenzo depended on minority grants and scholarships to get through law school. He wants to give something back."

Richard spoke up. "Sounds like he's on a mission, and you can't argue with morality. We do have a pro bono policy, but I don't think we've taken on too many cases in the past few years. If we offered him a chance to work in that venue, maybe we'd get that edge."

Paul cast him a disapproving glance. "We've gone over this before. Pro bono means we don't charge for the work. If we have unbillable hours structured into the day, we either decrease year-end bonuses or put in extra hours. Partners are averaging fifty-hour weeks and associates are at sixty plus. Are you suggesting we cut bonuses?''

Sara glanced quickly around the conference table, and saw nothing but scowls and blank expressions. No one was willing to bite *that* bullet.

Richard cleared his throat. ''On a lighter note, is it fair to say that whatever our Harvard hotshot did in Cancún, it must have blown Mac's socks off?''

Everyone laughed at the use of Lorenzo's office tag, and Sara gave a silent thanks to Richard for breaking the tension; it had been thick. ''Mac was impressed,'' she said. ''So was Aaron Brooks. He specifically asked for Lorenzo on the Shadow Star team.''

Pat let out a low, unladylike whistle. ''That clinches my vote. The firm billed Shadow Star Films over two million last year.''

Paul glanced pointedly around the conference table. ''I assume we all concur with Mac's decision.'' He studied his fingernails while he waited, then flashed a questioning look around the table again. ''Good. Since we're all here, let's talk strategy on our other offers, shall we?''

His tone was agreeable, but his look was not. Sara knew there was an undercurrent to this meeting. Paul liked to be in the power seat, and Mac had wrested that away from him—easily and expertly. And everybody else knew it, too. Mac's presence was in the room as much as if he were actually there.

"We've got twelve clerks and seven slots," Paul said with cool authority. "With one offer on the table, we're at eleven and six, which doesn't add or subtract from the equation. I'd like to assume a yes from Duran, but we have to plan for contingencies. If he declines, his offer goes to another clerk—putting our ratio at eleven-seven. Advantage back to us. Did Mac given Duran the usual two weeks to decide?"

Sara took a calming breath. She knew Paul wasn't going to like her answer. "No. He gave him a month."

"The young man knows he's in the driver's seat," Pat observed. "If he takes the month, then declines, we'll have already extended our other offers. Any clerk who gets one that late will know he's second string."

Paul shook his head. "I don't like it, but it was Mac's call."

The other attorneys talked in low, disgruntled tones, but Richard clasped his hands behind his head and smiled thinly. "You've got to hand it to him. Duran's got the world by the tail."

"He's worked for it," Pat noted sharply.

Richard bowed slightly, conceding her point.

Paul looked around the table, his face grim, then pushed his chair back and started to rise. "I assume everyone will do their best to get Duran on board."

"There's one more thing," Sara said before anyone had a chance to think about leaving. It was time to drop the other shoe. Nothing like a little added pressure at the end of a tension-filled meeting.

Paul sat back down. "What is it?"

"The terms of the offer."

Paul shrugged. "Our salaries are already five thousand above every other firm in the city."

Noting that Paul didn't mention his earlier suggestion of a signing bonus, Sara arched her brows and slowly scanned the room. "Mac wants to start him at seventy, with another five as a signing bonus."

The silence that followed was abruptly broken by the stunned voice of a junior partner. "That's what we're paying second-year associates."

Pat pushed her chair back and stood up. Her face was pale, but the tone of her voice clear and unequivocal. "I'm backing Mac's call, whatever the price."

"If Aaron Brooks wants Duran, that's good enough for me," Paul seconded tersely. "Is everyone agreed?" He glanced around the table and was met by brief nods and murmurs of agreement. He turned abruptly to Sara. "Have Duran's offer drawn up. I'll sign it tomorrow." With that, he got up and quickly left the room.

Sara picked up Lorenzo's personnel file, waited until everyone else had left, then followed them. Pat was waiting for her.

"Sara, can you give me a brief rundown on Kramer? How's he doing?"

"I'm not sure he's going to make the cut. Some things came up in Cancún—"

"That doesn't surprise me," Pat interrupted with a wave of her hand. "What about Anne Lockwood? I'm impressed with her work. And Bob Simms."

"I've heard the same from a few other partners, too. Anne looks like one of our top picks and Bob's on track, but a bit farther behind in the pack."

Pat gave her a thoughtful look. "I'll check with Bob. See what he's working on and if he needs any direction." A smile brightened her face. "It doesn't surprise me that Anne's doing well. She's very competitive. Ran me around a tennis court last week, and that was after we finished a big initial offering in corporate." She glanced at her watch. "It's after five and I've got a client waiting. Thanks for the update."

"No problem." Sara's day wasn't over yet either. She hurried down the hallway, already a few minutes late for a budget meeting with the VP of Finance.

A few days later, Lorenzo walked down San Pedro Street on his way to the immigration clinic in Oakland. Although he'd never been in the building, he'd passed it a hundred times over the years. It was only a few blocks from where he grew up, and a dozen in the other direction from the small second-floor apartment he'd rented.

Although his mother had wanted him to move home for the summer, his old bedroom was barely large enough for a twin bed and a small desk. Throughout high school and college he'd competed with his mother's tamales and frijoles for space on the kitchen table to open his books and study. As much as he enjoyed his mother's company, he also wanted his privacy.

He passed by buildings spray-painted with dirty streaks of red, yellow, and black graffiti, then turned the corner on to Sacramento. Halfway down the block he slowed when he saw the building and the people. The circa 1930s warehouse was built of brick, faded and worn with the years.

A sooty blanket of asphalt covered the area between the building and the cracked sidewalk. A chain-link fence ran the perimeter of the sidewalk, creating a dividing line between the people outside the system and those inside.

There were about a dozen people lined up on the sidewalk, all waiting patiently. Some stood in small groups, gesturing to one another with their hands as they talked. Others stood alone and were silent. He reminded himself that it was only nine o'clock in the morning and that, as the day wore on, so would their patience.

He passed through the fence, along the broken sidewalk and toward the front door. The first thing he noticed was the wrought-iron bars protecting the pane of glass set in the top half. Harsh, bitter memories coursed over him, but he let them come. Let them engulf him in an angry, bruising cloudburst of pain.

If he was to work here, if he was to make a difference, he had to remember. Everything. He had to remember the past, but more important, he had his eyes on the future.

He walked inside and was immediately flooded by noise. Impatient voices in foreign accents, children crying, telephones, the clatter of typewriters, and the more subtle noise of computer keyboards and printers. People occupied the couches and folding chairs in the waiting area; more leaned against the wall or sat on the floor.

He looked past them to see a half-dozen large wooden desks piled high with books and thick, rust-colored file folders. He noticed computer terminals on two of the desks, and typewriters on the others. Long fluorescent tubes on the ceiling flooded the room with light. People bustled everywhere, and the air was charged with intensity.

"Buenos días," a high-pitched voice rang through the commotion.

He turned to find a young woman sitting behind a desk separating the reception area from the rest of the building. She had curly black hair, wide eyes, and a snug little mouth painted dayglow pink. She was eyeing him curiously while fiddling with a pencil.

"Good morning," he replied, then watched as she

looked from his three-piece, pin-striped navy blue suit, all the way down to his polished shoes, then back. Her eyes held his for a fraction of a second, then she gave him a somewhat puzzled smile. "Can I help you?"

"Yes. I'm Lorenzo Duran and I'm—"

Her smile broadened. "Starting work here today."

He nodded. "That's right."

"Mr. Wagner is expecting you." She pointed toward the back of the room, where he counted three doors standing open. "First door on the left."

"Thanks." He made his way toward Mr. Wagner's office, checking things out along the way. Bookshelves and worktables stretched along one wall, and farther in, gray filing cabinets stood in groups of three as a buffer between desks. He noticed feathery green plants on several, and cacti on another. The carpet was nondescript brown and well worn. For the most part, the office seemed geared for work.

Everyone he saw wore either jeans or casual clothes, even those sitting behind desks. He noticed several people look up at him curiously as he walked by, and wondered if wearing a suit had been a mistake.

He stopped in front of Wagner's office and glanced in. A man sat behind the desk, leaning precariously on the back legs of a straight-backed chair. He appeared to be in his thirties, with a pale complexion and light brown hair. He wore faded jeans and a plaid cotton work shirt with the sleeves rolled up past his elbows.

This was the director? He cradled a telephone receiver in one hand while methodically rapping a pencil against the side of the desk with the other. He saw Lorenzo standing in the doorway, said a few words into the receiver, and hung up.

"Can I help you?" he asked, still leaning back in his chair.

"I'm looking for Mr. Wagner."

"You found him. What can I do for you?"

"Lorenzo Duran," he said, taking a step inside and extending his hand.

Wagner edged his chair to the floor, strode over, and grasped Lorenzo's hand. Then he took a step back, rested his hands on his hips, and gave Lorenzo an undecided once-over. "We open at eight."

Lorenzo caught himself before blurting out that Davis & MacGregor had started their workday at nine. That would have been a mistake. Instead, he said, "Sorry, sir. I'll be here before eight from now on."

Wagner nodded. "Good, and the name's Bud. Come on." He started out the door. "I'll show you around."

Lorenzo was introduced to everyone and everything in a couple of hours. The same routine had taken two days at Davis & MacGregor. Wagner also showed him how to operate the photocopy and fax machines, and how to make coffee. With a slight frown, Lorenzo realized he'd gotten quite used to having secretaries do all that for him.

He was even more startled when Bud gave him a preview of what to expect tomorrow—his first full day on the job: A crash course on basic immigration law, an overview of legal matters the clinic handled, and how to conduct an initial interview with a client, keep track of his time, and thread his way through a maze of paperwork. He'd also be interviewing clients and obtaining background information for the attorneys who actually handled the cases.

Bud stressed that Lorenzo would be the first one to ask the clients questions and, more important, the one they looked to for answers. Most clients came in nervous and scared. One of his jobs was to reassure them as best he could. Although Bud planned to sit in on his first few interviews, after that he was on his own.

By the end of the day Lorenzo's head was swimming, and when Bud suggested a beer before heading home, he readily agreed. They crossed the street to Miguel's Tavern and slid onto stools at the end of the bar. There was a dog-eared pool table at the back where one man chalked his cue and another racked brightly colored billiard balls.

"How would you sum up your first day?" Bud asked after ordering two drafts.

Lorenzo yanked his tie loose and ran two fingers around the neck of his starched white shirt. "Hectic. Challenging. Great."

Bud stared at him evenly, then drank half his beer in one long draw. "We operate differently from most firms. Some people adjust, others never do. You seemed nervous today, and a little slow on the up-take."

Lorenzo paled, then took a long drink. *Slow on the uptake?*

Bud shrugged. "Maybe it's only first-day jitters."

Lorenzo ran the back of his hand across his mouth. Was Wagner suggesting he didn't have what it took for the job? He had offers from the best firms in San Francisco—the thought was incomprehensible. "What do you mean?" he asked, his voice on edge.

"I'm sure you'll get the hang of things," Bud assured him. "But we're shorthanded and the clinic can be pretty intimidating. It's always hectic, and we usually cram twelve hours of work into ten on the clock."

Lorenzo looked him straight in the eye. If Wagner thought the clinic was intimidating, he didn't know him very well. And, he reasoned, Wagner *didn't* know him. Lorenzo intended to set him straight. "I don't have a problem with the hours or with anything else I've seen today."

Bud dipped his head. "Good."

"But I am a little surprised by the level of responsibility given to law clerks. This kind of work is usually done by lawyers."

"You're right there," Bud agreed. "But while

we're waiting for a few good lawyers willing to work for what amounts to law clerk pay in the big firms, some of our clients are facing some serious issues. We don't have time to wait.''

''I understand that,'' Lorenzo interjected. ''And I didn't mean—''

''In some ways,'' Bud interrupted, ''the clinic serves as a seriously underrated educational experience. The upside is that you'll learn more here in a month than in your first year at any of the firms in the City. The downside is that the clients pay the price.'' He gave Lorenzo a hard look. ''And I don't mean in fees—''

Lorenzo shook his head in understanding.

''—if you don't do a good job. We can't always correct mistakes quick enough to head off a crisis.''

''I'll—''

''You'll do your best,'' Bud interrupted again.

Lorenzo had to stop himself from talking over Bud's words to finish his sentence. Wagner was dictating, not discussing, and Lorenzo found his style irritating. But Wagner was in charge and style wasn't the issue. Lorenzo clenched his jaw and slanted his dark eyebrows in a frown.

''I'll give you as much direction as I can,'' Bud promised. ''But the more time I spend with you, the less I practice law. We've only got three attorneys on staff, and there's a backlog of appeals that would choke a Supreme Court Justice.''

"Appeals to stay in the country?"

Bud paused a minute before answering in a tired voice. "Contrary to popular belief, most of our clients are in the U.S. legally. Sure, we help some illegals. Mostly the ones who qualify to stay under the 1990 Amnesty Act."

"I'd have thought all those people were already processed."

"Not so. That was a good law, but there's a catch. If any children were born to the parents while they were in the country illegally, the kids don't qualify to stay."

Lorenzo narrowed his eyes, clearly puzzled. "I don't get it."

"The way the law reads, although the parents can stay, the kids get shipped back to wherever the parents came from."

"The government sends the children back alone? Without their parents?"

Bud shrugged. "Sometimes. I can usually get around it, but first I have to get the parents to come in. That's the first hurdle."

Lorenzo looked off in the distance, his mind in turmoil. He thought about how he'd feel if he were put in that position. A troubling thought about his father started to surface, but he quickly relegated it to the back of his mind. He didn't like to think about his father. He ran a hand over his face, then turned toward Bud. "I can't imagine what it would do to a man, having his children sent away. To not be able to bridge the thousand miles between them, with no hope of reunion.''

Bud's mouth twisted wryly and he tipped his glass to Lorenzo. ''That's where we come in.''

''How can I help?''

''By learning as fast as you can, and seeing as many clients as you can.''

Lorenzo nodded grimly.

''There's something else you can do.'' Bud gave Lorenzo an amused look. ''Leave the suit at home. It'll only get in the way.''

Chapter Six

The first few days blurred into a roller coaster of inspiration and discouragement, power and impotence as Lorenzo unraveled people's problems and tried to find solutions. The first time he had to tell a client he couldn't stay in the U.S., his gut twisted in a hard knot. The one thing he hadn't counted on was his emotional involvement with the clients. He found it impossible to respond any other way.

Late one afternoon, the receptionist asked if he had time to see a new client—one without an appointment. He looked past her to see an impressive man, about forty, dressed in what looked like a custom-tailored gray suit, French-cuffed shirt, and Gucci loafers. He could have stepped right out of *GQ*. Lorenzo's first thought was that he belonged across the Bay in San Francisco, not on the seedy side of Oakland.

"Jack Tarkington," the man's deep voice boomed as he shook hands, then sat in one of the straight-backed chairs in front of Lorenzo's desk. "I'd hoped to see an attorney, but I understand you've just finished your last year of law school."

"Yes. Harvard," Lorenzo announced bluntly, trying to put the man at ease. He had no doubt Tarkington usually dealt with a different economic stratum than most of their clients. Harvard might put them on an even plane.

When Tarkington blinked in surprise, then settled back in his chair, he knew he'd made his point.

"I'm interning at the clinic and handle initial interviews," Lorenzo explained. "You'll see a staff attorney next."

Tarkington nodded. "All right. I'm short of time, so let's get started. I need some legal advice. My wife died about two years ago, and I hired a woman to care for my three children." He paused, running a hand over his face. "Actually, I went through several. My wife's death was quite sudden, and it was a difficult time"

Lorenzo looked up from where he was writing. "That must have been hard on your children," he commented, giving Tarkington a moment to collect his thoughts.

"Yes. Rosa's been wonderful with the kids, and they adore her. She cooks, walks the kids home from school, and sits up with them when they're sick. She's become part of my family. A few weeks ago, Rosa came to me. Said she had a problem and needed my help."

Lorenzo looked up. He could tell from Tarkington's voice that he was obviously distressed.

"There isn't much I wouldn't do for her," he went on. "I could afford to hire the best attorneys in town, but I'm afraid Rosa's problem could hurt my business. I need this taken care of quietly."

"What's Rosa done?"

Tarkington's face grew angry, and he waved one hand in the air. "Nothing, as far as I'm concerned. She came up from Mexico a dozen years ago with her family. Her father had no job, and his kids were hungry. They crossed the border at night and never went back."

Lorenzo put down his pencil and sat back in his chair. "She's here illegally?"

Tarkington nodded.

"That could be a problem," Lorenzo acknowledged, then asked, "Is Rosa married?"

"Yes. Her husband was born right here in Oakland. Rosa doesn't have papers, and I want to know what I have to do to get this straightened out."

Lorenzo leaned forward and gave Tarkington an

encouraging look. "I'm sure we can help. And as for publicity, why would anyone care about Rosa?"

"Because I'm CEO for Harper & Ross," Tarkington said, his face grim. "We're the largest advertising firm in the Bay Area, and one of our clients is the city of San Francisco. I'm sure you've read newspaper accounts of government officials losing their posts because someone found out they'd had illegals working in their homes for years."

Lorenzo narrowed his eyes. "There was a story a few weeks ago—front page, as I recall."

Tarkington nodded sharply, and a flash of something—Lorenzo couldn't tell if it was embarrassment or resolve—crossed his face.

Tarkington shrugged. "Something tells me the city wouldn't appreciate a similar story involving a Harper & Ross executive splashed across the front page of the *San Francisco Examiner.*"

"I see your point." Lorenzo rested his hands on the narrow arms of his chair. "I don't think you have to worry about the press. They only come to this part of town if they're monitoring police radio frequencies."

Tarkington let out a relieved sigh. "That's what I'd hoped. Although I must admit I am concerned about the level of services you can give me. I don't mean to offend you, but Rosa deserves the best attorney available, and I'm not sure—"

"Just because the clinic serves the poor doesn't

mean we're substandard,'' Lorenzo interrupted, keeping his voice neutral. There was no point in taking offense. Tarkington was used to different surroundings. He understood that.

''The lawyers here know immigration law better than the firms downtown because they work it every day. And they care about people. Do you want help or not?''

''Yes, but—''

''I'm not a practicing attorney yet, but I know enough about immigration law to tell you Rosa has a good case. If she's married to a United States citizen, she'll only have to jump through a half-dozen hoops.''

''Such as?''

''She has to prove beyond a doubt that the marriage wasn't entered into on false pretenses, and she has to remain married for two years.''

''Is that all there is to it?''

Lorenzo smiled and shook his head. ''There's a lot more to it, but if she can't meet those criteria, there's no point in going any further. Will Rosa pass?''

''Absolutely. Her husband works for me too; he's my gardener. They've already been married two years, and Rosa just found out she's expecting their first child. That's why she finally came to me. She wants to get this straightened out before the baby's born.''

''I think we can do that.'' Lorenzo glanced at his

appointment calendar, then reached for a pen. "When can Rosa and her husband—" He glanced at Tarkington.

"Carlos Morales."

"When can they come in?"

Tarkington opened his hands. "How about tomorrow?"

Lorenzo pursed his lips into a thin line. "I'm booked solid. How about the next morning? Nine o'clock?"

"That'll be fine."

"The appointment will take about two hours. They'll need to bring their birth certificates, marriage certificate, and Carlos's passport if he has one."

Tarkington reached in his inside pocket for a slim notebook, and Lorenzo reached across his desk to hand him a pen.

"I'll need both their addresses for the last five years, the names of their nearest relatives, and employment information. We'll also need three or four people who can corroborate details of their marriage."

"What sort of details?"

"Things to prove it's a real marriage—people who've seen them together, who can testify that they hold hands, argue, kiss, and make up. And I'll interview Carlos and Rosa separately to compare answers to questions like"—he gestured with one hand—

"what time they get up, which side of the bed they sleep on. Little things that say they're a couple."

Tarkington smiled. "I don't think that will be a problem."

"Good." Lorenzo glanced at his watch. "There's another reason it's important to obtain Rosa's legal status as soon as possible. Since the baby will be born here, he'll automatically be a United States citizen, but if Rosa's picked up she could be forced to leave her child and return to Mexico. Eventually, we'd work it all out, but I'd hate to see the family split up, even for a few weeks."

The blood drained from Tarkington's face, and he slipped the notebook in his suit pocket. He started to get up, then sat back down and gave Lorenzo an assessing look. "I like how you do business, Mr. Duran. To the point. No mincing words. How'd you like to handle some other matters for me?"

Lorenzo gulped back his surprise and leaned his elbows on the worn arms of the chair. He tented his fingers together, hoping to look calm and collected, when his pulse was racing like a sprinter's in a hundred-yard dash.

"What did you have in mind, Mr. Tarkington?"

"Corporate work. Maybe some personal matters as well. I'd like to field some things your way that require some finesse. I have a feeling you'd be very good at that."

Lorenzo held out his hands, palms up. "I'm flattered, of course, but I'm afraid it's not possible. I'll be taking the bar exam in a few weeks and can't officially practice until I have the results."

An easy smile lit Tarkington's face. "I'm not worried about your passing the bar. Which firm will you be joining?"

Lorenzo didn't answer immediately, and Tarkington's brows shot up in surprise. "Surely you won't be working here. At the clinic."

"No." Lorenzo shook his head. "I don't expect so. I'm considering Davis & MacGregor."

Tarkington beamed his approval. "An excellent firm."

"If you'd like to discuss an association with Davis & MacGregor, I'm sure I could arrange an appointment with Mac MacGregor."

Tarkington tented his fingers together and gave Lorenzo an appraising look. "Only if you'll handle my accounts once you're there."

Lorenzo hesitated, knowing he couldn't give a definite answer. New associates worked directly under partners, and they would control his caseload. It made sense to him that he would work with any client he brought into the firm, but he couldn't be sure. There was a lot he didn't know about the firm's inner workings, but he did recognize an opportunity when he saw one, and this one came in the guise of Jack Tarkington.

He paused a moment and took a slow, even breath.

"Since I haven't officially joined the firm yet, of course I don't have authority to make decisions on behalf of the firm."

"Of course." Tarkington nodded, obviously waiting for Lorenzo to go on.

The lines of concentration deepened along Lorenzo's brow and around his eyes as he measured the man seated before him. "I would like to represent both you and Harper & Ross," he said in a guarded tone. "Working together, it's possible we can make that happen."

The beginning of a smile tipped the corner of Tarkington's mouth as he met Lorenzo's gaze. "I see," he said knowingly. "Perhaps I should talk directly with Mr. MacGregor?"

"I'll call your secretary once I've set up the meeting." Lorenzo stood and extended his hand. "I look forward to working with you."

Sara walked quickly toward Mac's office. She'd been interviewing a secretarial applicant when he'd called, and although he'd said it was important, she'd put him off until the interview was over. It was the end of the week and her secretary had called in sick three days in a row, then quit with no notice. She was desperate to replace her.

She stopped at Mac's open door and knocked. He looked up from where he sat working behind a massive, dark-grained mahogany desk and waved her in.

She closed the door and slid into a high-backed leather chair the color of warm butterscotch. A matching couch stood across the room, flanked by two chairs upholstered in rich, jewel-toned tapestry. Bookshelves filled with thick law books stretched ceiling to floor along one wall, and a dark antique table and four high-backed chairs were angled in one corner. Mac's office had the thick-carpeted, wax-shining amplitude of all the partners' offices. But there were subtle differences only someone in the business would recognize.

First, it was a corner office. Although Davis & MacGregor occupied three floors of the Hayworth Building, one was completely taken up by Accounting, Administration, Word Processing, and Information Systems. The library stretched across one end of the second floor, leaving only two corner offices, and there were the usual four on the third floor. That meant there were only six corner offices available to a firm of over a hundred lawyers. Occupying one spoke volumes about your position, prestige, and paycheck.

So did the number of windows. The associate attorneys, the Director of Personnel, and Sara, as Recruiting Administrator, had offices that were somewhat smaller, each with two windows. Senior associates merited larger offices with three windows, and partners had a bank of four. Corner offices had two banks of four.

She crossed her legs and smoothed the pleated skirt of her navy blue silk dress. She sat silent while Mac finished what he was writing, put his pen down, then leaned back in his chair. "I need your input on something," he said, sounding querulous and impatient.

Sara felt herself tense slightly. It wasn't like Mac to be so brusque. His expression was serious, and she was keenly aware of his scrutiny as he watched her.

"I've got to make some decisions," he announced, still staring at her. "And you may be able to help."

"Sure." She opened her hands. "What's up?"

"I saw a new client today." He stopped, pressed his lips together, then continued. "Anyway I hope he'll be a new client. Jack Tarkington, Chief Executive Officer of Harper & Ross, a major advertising firm with Fortune 500 clients from here to New York."

"Sounds good. What's the problem?"

"Lorenzo Duran."

Sara frowned. "What's he got to do with Tarkington?"

"I'm not sure, but it seems Tarkington wants Duran to represent him."

"But he hasn't taken the bar yet."

Mac shook his head vigorously. "Tarkington knows that, but he wants assurances that Duran will head up his team if he brings his business here."

Sara's frown turned to puzzlement. "We can't promise that. Lorenzo hasn't even accepted our offer yet. And when he does, he'll still be a first-year associate. He can't head up any team.''

''I explained all that to Tarkington, and he understands a partner has to be in charge, but he insists that Duran second-chair anything else. Says his cases will be good training ground.''

''Sounds like he knows Lorenzo pretty well. What's the connection?''

Mac pursed his lips into a thin line. ''I don't know. Tarkington talked around it, but never fully explained any connection. That's where I want your help.'' He gave Sara a sharp look. ''That and one other thing. I want Duran, and I want him now. It was a mistake to give him time to decide to come on board. I should have insisted he decide on the spot.''

''You didn't have much choice,'' Sara reminded him, discomfited by Mac's anger. ''His request wasn't unreasonable, especially since he has other offers.''

Mac waved one hand in the air. ''I don't care about his other offers,'' he said, his voice cold.

Sara blanched.

''As long as Lorenzo's on a long rope, anyone could step in and top our offer. I want Tarkington's business, and I need Duran to get it. I want you to find out what it'll take to get him to accept now.''

Sara sat calmly in the chair, her hands tensed together in her lap. Her self-control was a smoke screen. Inside, she was seething. Mac was trying to break an agreement with Lorenzo, and he was trying to use her to do it. Could she refuse and still keep her job? It took only a few seconds to decide the job wasn't worth the price. If he gave her no choice, she'd have to resign.

Her voice was cold and flat when she finally asked, "You're going back on your agreement?"

There was an almost imperceptible hardening to Mac's expression before he slowly stood and walked over to the mahogany bookshelves lining the wall. He leaned against the shelves, staring out the window at the skyline of downtown San Francisco. "This is a business decision, pure and simple." He turned back around and looked at her. When he spoke, his voice was remarkably calm. "You disappoint me, Sara. I thought you were loyal to the firm."

She took in a deep breath. "I am, Mac. I don't see that as the issue." She looked down at the thick, almond-colored carpeting, wishing she could bury herself in it. Mac had given her this job. Ultimately, she answered to him. She knew the one thing he wouldn't tolerate was disloyalty.

Mac slid his hands in his trouser pockets and rocked back on his heels. Then he gave a look that sent a chill through her. She recognized the steely-eyed look of ruthlessness that had enabled him to weather twenty years as head of the firm.

"Do as I ask, Sara," he said finally. "I believe that's your job."

She stood slowly, angling her chin in the air. "And if I disagree?"

Mac visibly flinched. "Are you saying you won't carry out my instructions?"

"I'm saying I have a problem with what you're asking me to do."

When he gave her an incredulous look, she realized she had only one avenue left to her. "Of course, I'll understand if you want me to resign."

Mac gave her a withering stare, shuttered his eyes briefly, and waved his hand. "Don't be ridiculous. That won't solve the problem. Sit down, Sara."

She did, keeping her back ramrod straight.

"You and I both know there are some who doubt your value to the firm, and the whole concept of recruiting, for that matter."

She nodded her agreement.

"And a few of the partners think I give you too much authority." He turned back to look out the window that spanned almost the entire east wall of his office. He had a postcard view of the Golden Gate Bridge spanning the Bay, its weblike golden girders turned orange by the setting sun.

She waited, watching Mac watch the spectacular view.

He turned back around and faced her. "I know better."

Relief poured over Sara at his words. She wouldn't have to resign.

''There's no question in my mind about your abilities, Sara. And up to now, I've never questioned your loyalty.'' He shook his head. ''I'm not sure what the problem is, but we both need to take a look at where we go from here.'' He absently glanced at a stack of file folders on his right, then picked one up and opened it. ''That's all for now, Sara.''

She left, speaking to no one as she walked down the hall and got on the elevator. When she reached her office, her gaze shifted from the mass of paperwork consuming the desk to the fading sunlight streaming through the window. Her thoughts of the last few weeks came back to her. Maybe the job did cost too much.

Lorenzo read the handwritten note forwarded to him from Davis & MacGregor, then set it on the desk next to the firm's offer letter. He still couldn't believe it. Seventy thousand to start and another five if he accepted in the next three weeks. He leaned back in his chair and anchored his hands behind his head.

The note was a dinner invitation from Aaron Brooks for the next time he traveled to San Francisco. On one hand, he was dining with movie moguls and contemplating a high-flying career; on the other, he was working at the immigration clinic and eating take-out pizza in front of the TV. It was hard to put his finger on which was real.

All he could think about was sleep. He'd gotten

home about nine, worked until eleven, then climbed into bed. After tossing and turning for another hour, he'd ripped the covers off the bed, gotten up, and slumped in a well-worn, comfortable chair. The moonlight coming through the window bathed the room in purple shadows and dark corners. He frowned out the window at the gray shadowed city outside, then stared at the telephone perched on the nightstand.

He couldn't get his mind off Sara.

He'd wanted to talk to her, tell her how the job was going, and talk about his offer from the firm. But it had been over a week and still he hadn't called.

He leaned over, picked up the phone, and dialed. When he heard her voice, he breathed easier. He'd told himself he only wanted to explain about the clinic, but he'd been lying to himself. He hadn't even realized it until he heard her voice, but what he really needed was to see her smile.

"Sara?" he said in a low voice. "Did I wake you?"

"Lorenzo?" She swallowed her sleepiness, then smiled through the darkness. She'd wanted to talk to him, but it had been more than that—she'd *needed* him. But after the meeting with Mac she'd almost been afraid to pick up the phone. She sat up in bed, switched on a small crystal boudoir lamp, then slit her eyes at the sudden jolt of light.

"I'm sorry I didn't call before, but with the new job my time's been tight."

"I understand." She hoped he wouldn't hear the catch in her voice. "How are you?" she asked, thinking it sounded stupid but not knowing what else to say.

He laughed softly. "My world turned upside down the day I walked in the clinic door. I always knew law was what I wanted to do, but I never expected it to have such an effect. It's tough, but it's gotten under my skin."

She lay back against the pillow, his enthusiasm catching her so off guard she forgot all about her problems. "It sounds exciting. Tell me more."

He hesitated, wanting to see her but not wanting to break the spell of their conversation. Finally, he said, "It's hard to talk on the phone. How about trying it in person?"

Her eyes widened. "Now?"

He laughed. "No. How about dinner. Tomorrow night."

"Okay. As long as it's not too early. I'm interviewing a secretary at five."

"I've got a late appointment too. I could meet you about eight. Eduardo's on Forty-third and Taylor is close, and the food's good if you don't mind the drive."

"Not at all. I'll see you then." Sara hung up the phone, pulled the sheets up to her chin, and wondered what had prompted him to call. She decided it didn't matter.

* * *

Sara glanced at her watch again, then frowned. She'd arrived at the restaurant at eight, and it was now half past. Where was he? It was difficult enough to just sit there, twirling the thin red straw she'd plucked from her wine spritzer, but it was embarrassing to occasionally catch the eye of other diners, knowing they wondered why she was there alone—and, as time went by and she kept glancing at her watch, whether she'd been stood up.

Why else would a woman sit alone in a candlelit restaurant and not order dinner? She looked like she was waiting for someone, and she was. Her dress was pale yellow silk, with a full belted skirt and V-neck that dipped low. She'd swept her hair to one side and anchored it with a silver comb shaped like a seashell.

She was all dressed up, and she'd been stood up.

She waved at the waiter hovering nearby, and discreetly tucked a ten-dollar bill under her empty plate. It was Friday night, she was taking up a table, and the waiter was losing tips. He had every reason to hover, and to wonder how long she'd wait before giving up and leaving.

Just then, the maitre d' appeared at her elbow and placed a telephone on the table in front of her. "Ms. Jackson, there's a call for you."

She gave him an uncertain look, then gingerly picked up the receiver. There was only one person who knew where she was.

"Lorenzo?"

"Thank god you're still there."

"Yes. Where are—"

"I'm sorry," he interrupted. "But I'm in the middle of an emergency, and—"

She felt the blood siphon out of her face. "Are you all right?"

"Yes, I'm fine, but I'm still at the clinic."

Sara felt her pulse lurch. "What happened?"

"Immigration picked up two children today and—" His voice broke, then he went on. "It's a long story, Sara, but the bottom line is the office staff has all gone home, and I need some help. Are you game?"

Sara spoke quickly into the phone. "Of course. What can I do?"

"Come to the office. It's on Sacramento and Fourth. There's a parking lot next to the clinic. I'll go outside in ten minutes to meet you."

Within an hour, Sara was pulling forms out of filing cabinets and typing affidavits while Lorenzo maneuvered between phone calls and talking with a quiet, middle-aged couple who spoke very little English. At this point, Sara figured she could help most by inputting data on the computer or helping pull cases. She also knew enough about citations to find the right books once they started working on the legal brief.

"How did all this happen?" she asked when Lorenzo brought her some notes to type. "Two children picked up off the street when hoodlums run free?"

He gave her a sharp look. "The government only needs a small excuse to put you away, and in this case they have what most people would consider a good reason—the kids are here illegally."

"But they're just children," she argued adamantly. "It doesn't make any sense."

He threw out his hands. "That's exactly why I'm here—to try and make sense of the situation. I hope to have them back by morning." Lorenzo ran a tired hand through his hair, then paced a few feet away.

He nodded toward the couple, their heads close together, sitting in straight-backed chairs at the conference table. "They were some of my first clients. They'd come from San Jose to find out how to become legal residents. They could have applied years ago, but they were scared. When they finally saved up enough money to bring their children here from Mexico, they decided to make a move." He let out a big breath.

"But I don't get it. Why were the kids picked up?"

"They were in the wrong place at the wrong time. Seems they turned a corner and ran into a street fight about the same time the cops showed up." He shrugged. "They pretended not to speak English, so they were brought in."

"Why did they do that?"

"Fear."

She nodded, grim faced.

He made a slight dismissive gesture with his right

hand. ''I didn't learn much about immigration law at Harvard. And as it is, I'm having to learn the hard way.'' He gave her a knowing glance. ''On-the-job training.''

A smile moved over her face. ''You love it, don't you?''

''Yeah.'' He nodded emphatically. ''And I think I can make a difference. That's the best part.''

Both turned at the sound of the front door opening and closing loudly. It was Bud.

''All right.'' Lorenzo let out a breath that was a mixture of both relief and anticipation. ''Now we'll kick into high gear.''

Chapter Seven

A few hours later, Lorenzo bent down next to Sara and studied her computer screen. "How are you doing on those last revisions?"

She gave him a skeptical look, then glanced at her watch. "*Last* revisions? I heard that one around midnight."

He immediately hunkered down next to her, a look of concern turning his features serious. "I'm sorry, Sara. But this brief is important. I've got to persuade the judge—"

She reached out and gently touched his arm. "Calm down. I was just kidding." When he didn't respond, just stared at her, she ran her fingers down his arm, stopping just below where his shirtsleeve met his bare skin. "Lorenzo?"

119

Still he remained silent.

"Is anything wrong?"

He looked deliberately at where her hand rested against his skin. When he looked at her, a rush of emotion crossed his face. She didn't know what he was thinking, but whatever it was, she felt the warmth of it all the way to her toes. The feeling scared her. Slowly, she pulled her hand away.

"I said I was only kidding," she whispered hoarsely.

"Yeah." He blew out an exaggerated breath and wiped his brow. "I knew that." A look of amusement lit the corners of his mouth as he stood, turned around, and leaned against her desk. When he tilted his head forward, a lock of black hair fell across his forehead. "You know, this is one heck of a first date."

Her gaze met his as the word *date* danced through her mind. She hadn't thought of it in quite that way, but who was she kidding? That's exactly what this was. He'd invited her out to dinner. She'd accepted. She'd broken her one cardinal rule—never date lawyers.

Just because the evening had turned into something else didn't make any difference. A second after she told herself she should run as fast as she could, a little voice insisted she was making too much out of a dinner invitation.

She was overreacting. She shouldn't let the past

interfere with the present. That was a problem she needed to correct and, as the old saying goes, there's no time like the present. Leaning back in her chair, she moved her hands behind her head and clasped them together. "You know, you're right. And the best part is"—she smiled up at him—"I'm having a good time."

He grinned widely, reached out, and lightly traced the line of her jaw with his index finger. "So am I." His eyes darkened as he searched her face. "But then I knew I would."

A rush of pink stained her cheeks, and she tried to ignore the knot forming in the pit of her stomach. The longer he looked at her the worse it got. Finally, she could no longer ignore the truth. The pull between them was growing stronger every day, and both knew it. So far, they hadn't talked about how they felt. It was almost like they'd entered into a pact of silence. She wondered who would be the first to break the unspoken truce.

Some time later, Bud carefully stacked the documents in his briefcase, then glanced across the conference table. Lorenzo sat back on the edge of one chair, his feet propped on the end of the table. Sara sat next to him, hunkered forward with her elbows on the table, her chin resting in both hands. "You two look exhausted," Bud said. "You better get some sleep."

Sara glanced at her watch. "Four-thirty! I had no idea it was that late. We've been working all night."

Bud nodded. "I'm just glad the judge agreed to an emergency hearing this morning. Can you imagine how long this night's been for the kids? They must be scared to death."

Sara blanched. Was he scolding her? She let out a long breath, briefly closed her eyes, and told herself she was overreacting. "I wasn't complaining," she assured him. "I'm just tired."

Lorenzo frowned, looking from Bud to Sara, then back again. "If it hadn't been for Sara, we still wouldn't be finished. She's been a lifesaver."

"Well said." Bud snapped his briefcase shut and caught Sara's eye. "We couldn't have done it all without you, Sara. Thanks for pitching in."

Lorenzo pushed his chair back and stood. "Another thing, Bud."

"What's that?"

"I'd like to attend the hearing."

"I was planning on it. You've put together some persuasive arguments and case law that should win our case. Besides, I need my second-chair in court."

Sara watched the expression on Lorenzo's face change in that scant second or two. His eyes shuttered briefly; his shoulders visibly straightened. When his eyes opened again, they flashed with . . . something. She couldn't put her finger on exactly what it was, but he looked different. Stronger, although she wouldn't have thought that possible. Maybe it was enthusiasm or a renewed sense of fulfillment.

Whatever it was, life burned brighter and hotter in some people, and Lorenzo was one of them. All the weeks he'd worked at the firm she hadn't seen him look quite that way. With a skittering heart, she suddenly realized it was quite possible Davis & Mac-Gregor might lose him.

Bud turned to Sara. "You're welcome to come along if you have an interest."

"I'd like that," she said, then let out a long breath. "But if I don't get a few hours' sleep I'll never make it. Would you mind if I napped on one of the couches in the reception room?"

Bud glanced sharply at Lorenzo. The two men exchanged a look that even Sara didn't misinterpret. What had she been thinking? She couldn't stay there alone; the clinic was in one of the worst neighborhoods in Oakland.

Lorenzo gave an exaggerated yawn, then ran a tired hand through his hair. "I could use some shut-eye myself."

"Good." Bud lifted his briefcase off the table. "You can keep each other company. "I'm going to head home. I've got to clean up before court." He glanced sharply at the dark shadow covering the lower half of Lorenzo's face. "And you need a shave."

Lorenzo ran a hand over his chin.

"Shaving gear's in the bottom right hand drawer of my desk. If you're lucky, I may even have a new razor."

Lorenzo gave him a wan smile. "Thanks."

Bud glanced at the law books strewn across the table. "Bring these with you in the morning. I've got copies of the petition, the brief, and the order we prepared for the judge's signature." He arched his brows. "Hopefully, he'll sign it as presented."

"And the kids will be back with their parents tomorrow," Lorenzo added.

"Right." Bud turned toward the door, then called over his shoulder, "See you in a few hours."

Lorenzo walked over to the sofa, pulling his rumpled shirt out of the waist of his pants as he went. He sat heavily, leaned forward, and started untying his shoes. Sara glanced down at the yellow silk dress she'd been wearing since leaving home last night—over eight hours ago. With a start, she realized she'd be wearing the same dress to court.

She grimaced, then brushed her hand back and forth across the skirt in an attempt to smooth out the web of wrinkles marring the delicate fabric. Just as quickly, she let out a long sigh and stopped her frantic movements. In a few minutes, she'd be sleeping in this dress. What was the point?

She looked up and met Lorenzo's gaze. He drew his lips in thoughtfully. "I've got clean sweat pants and a T-shirt if you'd like to change."

She closed her eyes. "I'd die for comfortable clothes."

"Now don't do that." He smiled, tossed his shoes to one side, and got up. As he walked past her, he ran his fingers along her arm. "I want you with me tomorrow."

Surprise siphoned the blood from her face, and she blinked several times. "You do?"

He reached his desk, bent down, and opened a bottom drawer. "Yeah," came a muffled reply, then he grabbed some clothing and shut the drawer with his foot. He walked back, holding out a white T-shirt and soft gray drawstring pants in one hand.

After she took the clothes, he lowered his hands to his sides and studied her. He seemed thoughtful, as though he were looking through and beyond her to something or somewhere else. She wondered what it was he saw, what he was thinking.

"I want you with me," he said finally in a sure, calm voice. "Because we make a damn good team."

A slight flush stained her cheeks. "Yes," she agreed softly. "I guess we do."

Two long tables the color of mahogany stood side by side a dozen feet in front of the judge's podium. A court reporter was seated to the left of the judge, a clerk to his right. Bud and Lorenzo sat behind one of the wooden tables, legal tablets, pens and several file folders open in front of them. A half dozen law books were stacked nearby, each marked with slips of paper in several places.

The attorney representing the INS sat at the second table. One slim file folder lay on the table in front of him.

Sara sat in the first row of seats, next to the children's parents. There were probably thirty people in the room, mostly attorneys or people waiting for their cases to be heard. The atmosphere was hushed, and when people did talk, they whispered behind their hands. Most stared silently at the judge as he glanced through files and documents. His high-backed leather chair was positioned on a platform a good five feet higher than the floor. The room had stately twelve-foot ceilings; the public seating area was lined with long wooden benches with high backs. The similarity to a church was striking.

Sara had been in court often while working for Davis & MacGregor, but the clients had been faceless multinational corporations. This was different. This case involved people's lives. She could see getting caught up in the law when you could help people. And if Lorenzo had come to love this work, she must have been wrong about him. He wasn't so caught up in his career that he'd let it take over his life.

Sara glanced to where Lorenzo sat next to Bud, wishing she could hold on to him while the judge rendered his verdict. Suddenly his shoulders seemed very broad. It occurred to her that Lorenzo was the kind of man you could depend on, the kind of man who'd make it through anything. Hadn't he proved that, just being in this courtroom?

She thought the case had gone well. Both children had testified. Their fear had been palpable, their voices strained as they answered questions, sometimes with the aid of an interpreter. It had been easy to believe they'd been so afraid of the police they'd remained silent. The arresting officer lacked any evidence they'd been involved in any crime, just that they'd refused to cooperate.

The judge cleared his throat, breaking the silence that hung over the courtroom like a somber cloud. He looked down from the bench, peering over rectangular half-glasses that did little to disguise his need for bifocals. He leaned forward in his chair and spoke directly to Bud.

"I've read your brief. The cases you've cited are on point." He switched his gaze to the attorney representing the INS and opened his hands. "I've gone over the police report and listened to the officer's testimony. I don't see the probable cause for bringing the minors in, let alone detaining them overnight. Have you got anything else?"

The attorney stood and smoothed his jacket.

"Your Honor, the evidence reflects that the minors refused to give any information at all, including their names. It took several hours to obtain even a phone number." He raised his voice. "The minors were in the vicinity of a crime, refusing to testify, and, as we have shown, are in the country illegally. We see no reason to hold them any longer, but we do request they be returned to their legal residence in Mexico.''

The judge looked to Bud. ''And the parents had already sought legal advice to correct the residence problem?''

Bud pushed his chair back and stood. ''Yes, Your Honor. They had met with my associate, Mr. Duran''—he gestured toward Lorenzo—''the week before the incident in question.''

The judge glanced at the paperwork in front of him. ''Mr. Duran's affidavit states he asked them to get some paperwork together, made a few calls on their behalf, and scheduled a second interview.'' He peered intently over the rims of his glasses. ''Mr. Duran?''

Lorenzo stood. ''Your Honor, I would add that the parents called to confirm their appointment. They were doing everything possible to correct the situation.''

''Were the children in school?'' the judge asked.

''No, Your Honor.''

The judge frowned.

Bud swiveled his head sharply toward Lorenzo.

Lorenzo kept his gaze on the judge. ''Your Honor, my clients didn't enroll the children in school because they didn't feel they had the right to receive benefits from the State of California.''

The judge gave an almost imperceptible nod, although his frown remained.

"The parents were teaching the children at home"—Lorenzo opened his hands in a gesture of entreaty—"and doing their best with a home schooling program, even though English is their second language. They felt it was a matter of honor to teach the children themselves."

The judge leaned back in his chair and glanced at the two children, then at their parents. He picked up his pen and announced loudly, "I'm going to release the children to their parents"—he glanced at the INS attorney—"and order that the record of their detention be expunged." He finished writing his name and looked at his watch. "Let's adjourn for fifteen minutes."

The clerk rapped a gavel twice and called out "All rise" as the judge left the courtroom.

Lorenzo turned and met Sara's glance. The smile on her face sent a warm glow through him. Without thinking, he closed the short distance between them. As he reached her, he opened his arms.

Sara felt as if it were the most natural thing in the world, stepping into his embrace, having his arms close around her. Feeling the texture of his jacket against her cheek, breathing in the musky fragrance of aftershave.

And just as suddenly, they moved apart.

Lorenzo's dark eyes widened in astonishment.

Sara stared back wordlessly.

What were they doing? They were in a courtroom! The look on his face told her he was thinking the same. Her breath caught in her lungs as she gulped air. "Congratulations." Her voice broke and she pressed her hand to her throat, glancing around to see if anyone was watching.

He plowed a hand through his thick hair, looking quickly to where Bud stood talking to the clients, then back to Sara. "I don't know what . . ." He opened his hands wide. "Well, I do, but this isn't the time"—he looked around again—"or the place."

Sara swallowed nervously.

"I want to talk to my clients." He glanced over his shoulder. "And Bud."

"And I need to get home," she blurted out nervously. "And I could really use a nap. Give Bud my best." She pressed her hand to his arm. "You both did a brilliant job."

"Thanks." He reached out, caught her hand, and gave it a squeeze. "I still owe you that dinner."

She arched one brow wickedly and gave him a playful look. "Yes, you do." She made a production of pulling her hand away, then wagging her index finger in front of his face. "And I intend to collect."

He grinned. "I'm counting on it."

Thursday evening Sara sat on the passenger side of the car, wondering how she was going to get through the next few hours. Lines creased her brow as they drove down Fourteenth Street. Then she crossed her arms and glowered.

She was angry.

She thought she knew Lorenzo, but she'd been wrong. They'd played phone tag several times, leaving messages that were answered by other messages, but they'd talked only once since the court hearing. He'd asked her out to dinner.

Fine.

In fact, terrific.

He hadn't mentioned any particular restaurant, but she hadn't cared. Still didn't. That had been her big mistake. After they got in the car, she casually asked where they were going. The last place she'd expected to hear was his mother's. It wasn't that she *minded* meeting his mother. It had just been such a . . . *surprise*.

And then he'd apologized, saying he tried to have dinner with his mother at least once a week, but his job had kept him working late every night. Of course, he'd offered to call and cancel; that had only made Sara feel guilty and selfish. How could you get mad at a guy who made a point of visiting his mother every week?

When they turned onto San Fernando, Lorenzo glanced out the front window. "This is the old neighborhood. Where I grew up."

She saw small apartment complexes and old houses

in need of paint surrounded by straw-colored grass and weeds. Some houses had chain-link fences, others thick, black bars over the windows and outlining small front porches. She saw a woman in a brown dress standing inside a barred porch carrying on an animated conversation with two teenagers standing on the other side of the bars. She wondered if they were her own children.

Lorenzo glanced toward her. "Not much to look at."

Sara met his gaze. She hesitated, running her tongue over her lower lip. "No wonder you wanted out."

He twisted his mouth into a cynical smile and looked back out the windshield. "That's putting it mildly."

Sara noticed the houses were starting to look neater. There were still bars on the windows, but the yards were green, a few with flowers edging the sidewalks and fences. She couldn't help but think how far Lorenzo had come. Being an attorney was a world away from this place, especially if he joined Davis & MacGregor.

"Just think," she said in a pensive voice. "Now that you've finished law school, and with all your job offers, you won't ever have to come back here."

When he didn't say anything, Sara realized she'd put her foot in her mouth.

"I'm sorry. I didn't mean—"

He gave her a sidelong glance. "This place will always be part of me."

"Of course. I just meant you don't have to come here anymore."

He let out a long breath, then stopped the car. He slid his right arm along the top of the seat, looked over his shoulder, and started backing the car into a parking place. "I do until I can convince my mother to leave."

Unconsciously, her brow furrowed. "I don't understand. Why would she want to stay?"

"She's lived her life here," he reasoned quietly. "I'd like to think I could give her a new life, but so far I haven't been very successful."

Sara waited patiently for him to walk around and open the door for her. They'd already had that argument when they'd driven to the courthouse. Though she'd been the one driving, he'd insisted on opening the door for her. That meant she had to sit and watch him walk around the front of the car when she could have easily gotten out all by herself. He'd even held out his hand to help her out of the car. The whole thing seemed awkward, but if it made him feel good to be chivalrous, who was she to argue?

It had nothing to do with competence or status, it only had to do with her being a woman. And him being a man. And that worried her, too.

She glanced out the car window at a beige two-story building with dark brown trim. A few tricycles and brightly colored toys were scattered around the rectangular, pale green lawn. Tall, straggly trees stood at the far end of the lot and a row of leafy shrubs lined the front. She also noticed several bicycles with heavy chains wound through their spokes, locking them to pipes coming out of the buildings.

Sara felt her nerves humming as she got out of the car. By the time they reached the front door, her pulse skittered. She chided herself for being silly, but the situation reminded her of times she'd brought guys home from college to meet her parents—and to pass inspection. And, she repeatedly told herself, that wasn't what was going on here.

The trouble was, she didn't exactly know what was.

He opened the door and swept her inside. Her first impression centered around evocative smells. Images of Cancún flooded over her as she took in a long, deep breath. Hot Mexican spices, cilantro, and chile peppers. Her mouth started to water. She suddenly realized she was starving.

Her second impression was that of welcome. The furniture looked comfortable, the drapes and matching slipcovers bright and cheery. Books and knickknacks lined white-painted shelves, and photographs decorated the walls. This wasn't an apartment—it was a home.

"Mamá," Lorenzo called loudly.

A small woman with a cap of black curly hair appeared at a doorway off the living room. She wore a blue-and-white checked dress and a frilly apron around her waist. She smiled at Sara, then opened her arms wide to Lorenzo. "You are late," she scolded.

"Yes, *mamá*. There was traffic." He hugged her briefly, then stepped aside and opened one arm toward Sara. "This is Sara. My mother, Maria."

Sara dipped her head slightly. "Mrs. Duran. I'm so glad to meet you."

Maria clucked her tongue. "You will call me Maria." She smiled brightly. "Come in the kitchen; we can talk while I cook."

"It smells wonderful!"

"*Bueno!* You aren't one of those skinny girls who don't like food, are you?"

Lorenzo threw his head back and laughed. "*No, mamá*. Sara has a good appetite."

"Then you will help me cook."

Sara swallowed hard. She'd never had time to cook—or the inclination to learn. She usually grabbed a carton of yogurt for breakfast and depended on take-out or restaurants for lunch and dinner. "Of course," she managed a feeble reply, "I'll be glad to help."

Ten minutes later, Sara was up to her knuckles in tomatoes, onions, peppers, and cilantro. She was making her first batch of salsa. The kitchen was hot, and her bangs kept getting in her eyes. She reached up and pushed the strands back from her face, then went back to chopping.

Maria peered inside the oven for a second or two,

then closed the white enamel door. She picked up a large wooden spoon, checked the green tomatillos to see if they were done, then stirred a pot of beans on the back burner of the stove. "I'm ready to refry the beans." She looked over her shoulder at Sara. "How's the salsa coming?"

Sara cupped the last of the onions in her hands and dumped them in the bowl, then glanced through the bangs that continued to fall over her eyes. She pushed at them again. "Everything's chopped. What comes next?"

Maria moved next to her. "Salt, pepper, and cumin," she said, picking up small jars and shaking them over the bowl.

"I could set the table," Sara suggested hopefully.

"Lorenzo!" Maria shouted. "Set the table, *por favor*." She moved a large cast-iron frying pan to the front burner, poured in a few tablespoons of oil, then retrieved a package of bacon from the refrigerator. "Can you chop a few pieces for the refried beans?" She handed the package to Sara and turned back to the stove.

Sara set her knife on the cutting board, pulled the package apart, and grabbed several long slices of bacon. Her eyes were smarting from onion and pepper juice. She sniffed, then rubbed her knuckles along the edge of her eyelid where tears threatened. As she peeled the bacon strips off the paper, her still-wet fingers skidded off the bacon strips and the package went flying. She let go of the bacon and grabbed at the package just as Lorenzo walked into the kitchen.

"Whoa!" He reached for the package, but it slipped through his hands and hit the floor.

Sara grimaced, rubbing at her eyes. "I'm sorry."

Maria glanced from Sara to Lorenzo, then shook her head in dismay. She swept the bacon strips off the floor and into the garbage can. Then she whipped out four more in one movement. "I'll finish here. Sara, why don't you wash up and give Lorenzo a hand." She smiled kindly. "Women always set a pretty table."

Sara wiped her eyes again, sighed, turned, and left the kitchen.

Once she'd left, Lorenzo met his mother's gaze. After a few seconds, he shook his head and chuckled.

"Your Sara, she does not cook?"

"Apparently not." A flash of humor crossed his face. "But she's got paperwork down to a science."

Maria went back to her stove. She was disappointed. When Lorenzo had asked to bring Sara to dinner, she thought the relationship must be serious. But this young woman didn't know the first thing about preparing a meal. Not even salsa!

She was obviously more interested in her job than getting married and having babies. And Lorenzo had told her not to worry about him anymore. Ha! He had the worst kind of trouble and didn't even know it.

Chapter Eight

Next to Maria Duran, Sara felt inadequate. Maria was an accomplished cook, her home gleamed—even the tile in the bathroom shone. Then there were her sewing skills—curtains, slipcovers, clothes for herself and four grandchildren. All that and she worked full time. The topper had been hearing about Maria's program teaching inner-city children to knit. And not just little girls—rambunctious boys, too. Who would have guessed that learning to knit could increase attention span *and* help with math and dexterity skills?

When Sara compared Maria's energy and commitment to her own, she came up lacking. All she produced were excuses. For not renovating her house, seriously pursuing basket weaving, or the dozen other things she kept telling herself she wanted to do. She ended up wondering if she was serious or just fooling herself.

The rest of the week she'd poured herself into a frenzy of activity, leaving the office at six, then dashing home to strip layers of faded paper off the downstairs walls. That gave her plenty of time to think about Lorenzo and the dilemma over her job. Should she try and persuade Lorenzo to accept the firm's offer? Should she tell Mac how Lorenzo felt about the immigration clinic? What was the best way to go about getting an assistant? She didn't have answers, but she did have plenty of questions.

And she had made one important decision. She'd met with Mary Dodd, the owner of the gallery where she'd successfully shown her baskets a few years ago. Mary was enthusiastic about showing her work again and commissioned two baskets for an upcoming exhibit on artistry of the American West.

She'd spent Sunday researching possible patterns, finally deciding on a coiled, cedar bark basket inspired by the Klickitat Indians of the Pacific Northwest. Originally used as trade items, the baskets were made of aged cedar bark and wheat-colored bear grass. She finished some preliminary sketches and found a supplier near Hood River, Oregon, for the bear grass. She prided herself on authenticity, and that meant going to the source.

The sound of the phone startled her, but a few seconds later Lorenzo's voice filled her with an immediate sense of comfort. She thought it peculiar that a man who caused her such turmoil could also have such a calming effect.

She listened as he described a case he was working on, then drew her brows into a frown. There was a familiar ring to this conversation she found unsettling. "It's Sunday," she interrupted. "Why are you at work?"

She stared up at the ceiling as he defended his seven-day-a-week schedule. She knew where she'd heard almost these same words—from her ex-husband. "The clinic isn't paying you enough to spend all weekend working," she argued, slipping her glasses off to rub at the bridge of her nose. She listened to him explain why he'd given up both Saturday and Sunday to work, but when he asked about Davis & MacGregor, she drew the line. She wouldn't be drawn into that conversation.

"That subject's off limits," she said, her voice quarrelsome. "I promised myself not to think about the office today. Surely there's something else we can talk about."

He apologized, and in another minute, she perked up. "*Quinceañera?* What's that?" She twirled the phone cord around her index finger as she listened to him describe his goddaughter Laura's coming-of-age party.

"Reminds me of a sweet sixteen party, only everybody and their cousins are invited." She glanced up at the high ceiling, thoughtful. "Since I come from a small family, a hundred people seems like a lot to me."

She leaned back in the chair and stretched her legs out in front of her. "Sounds like quite an evening. Thanks. I would like to go." She pushed herself into a sitting position. "See you Saturday. Meanwhile, don't work too hard."

After saying good-bye, she placed the receiver back on the cradle. She sat quietly for a few minutes, thinking about her life and whether she was making sound decisions. She was fully aware how some people let their emotions rule their lives; she didn't want to be one of those people. She wanted reason and logic in her life. That meant figuring out where she wanted to go, rather than drifting wherever circumstance took her. And that meant taking a long, hard look at both her job and her personal life.

In the meantime, she had to decide what to wear Saturday night. She climbed the stairs and went into her bedroom, reminding herself to decide on a color scheme for the large, airy room—just one more thing she wanted to do and couldn't seem to find the time for. She entered the walk-in closet and ran her hand over a dozen cocktail dresses. There were glimmering gowns with sequins and seed pearls, smooth satins, and sheer opaque silks. She had dresses in every color of the rainbow, but they were all wrong.

She took out several designer suits, but quickly replaced the hangers over the closet rod. This was a party, not a business affair. She glanced at her watch, wondering if her mother might be interested in going shopping one night later this week.

Thursday, her mother arrived at Davis & MacGregor at five sharp and dragged Sara out of the office. Downtown San Francisco had dozens of shops around Union Square, all within walking distance. They roamed the aisles in Saks and Bloomingdale's, then hit a few of the small and very expensive shops on Maiden Lane. Sara couldn't find anything.

At her mother's insistence, she finally agreed to visit Roberto Celan's couture salon. Celan was a new Italian designer who believed in simple lines and exquisite fabric. She scrutinized a sleeveless raw silk dress decorated with a single band of seed pearls along the scooped neckline. The skirt was slim and short. She held it up in front of her, then turned to her mother. "This emerald green is exquisite. And it's on sale."

Her mother glanced from the green sheath to the high-waisted, sapphire blue dress with matching jacket she'd just found. "What about this one, dear. I've always thought blue was more your color."

Sara shook her head. "Too dressy."

Her mother cocked her head to one side. "You could be right. How about the white wool?"

Sara narrowed her eyes, glancing from one dress to

the other. "It is beautiful, but Lorenzo's goddaughter may wear white. Guests aren't supposed to wear white to a wedding. Wouldn't the same rule apply here?"

Her mother arched her brows, took the dress, and put it back on the rack. "You may be right."

Sara let out a long breath. "Down to two." Her glance moved from one dress to the other. "I can't decide."

Her mother placed one hand on her hip and gave Sara a skeptical look. "You've never been one to worry about fashion." She paused dramatically. "Is there anything you'd like to tell me?"

Sara blushed. "I don't know what you mean."

"I mean . . ." Her mother threw out her hands. "Is this new man why you're so flustered?"

Sara's blush reddened. "I'm not flustered. And Lorenzo isn't a *new man.*" She glared at her mother. "I've already told you that."

"Yes you have." Her mother's mouth twitched in amusement. "And I don't believe you."

Sara gave her mother a scathing look, then ran a nervous hand through her hair. "I don't know. Maybe it's work."

"Hrumph! That's nothing new. You work at a firm like Davis & MacGregor and work will always be on your mind. I shouldn't have to tell you that. No." She shook her head. "Something else is bothering you."

Sara paused, trying to put into words the thoughts

that had occupied her mind for the last week. They were all jumbled together and didn't seem to be leading anywhere. Maybe her mother could help.

"I've always thought I knew what I wanted," she started carefully. "A career that gave me a sense of satisfaction and accomplishment."

"You've always needed a challenge, Sara. Your father and I knew that early on."

"The firm has given me that, but . . . I don't know, lately I've begun to question whether I'm good at my job."

Her mother's mouth dropped. "Whatever's gotten into you? You're extremely competent. Mac wouldn't keep you around if you weren't."

Sara gave her a wry look. "Right now I don't feel my job is exactly *secure*."

Her mother's glance turned sharp. "Why? Has something happened?"

"Nothing . . . unexpected," Sara finally answered. "I'm just not sure I want to do this long-term."

Her mother shrugged. "Nothing wrong with that. Are you thinking of changing careers?"

"Maybe, but I'm just not sure. I've got a college education, but what practical skills do I have?" She counted off on each finger. "Good verbal skills, my writing's clear and concise—"

"You're very organized and work very well with other people," her mother finished proudly.

Sara gave her a slight smile. "And I multitask really well."

"Multitask?"

"Do more than one thing at a time," Sara went on with a wave of one hand. "Usually two or three, and manage to keep them all separate."

Her mother gave her a small, dubious look.

Sara shrugged. "I'm just not sure those traits add up to anything of lasting value. I mean, a lot of people could handle my job. Sometimes I think I'd like to chuck it all and make a go of my basketry, or interior design. I do have a knack for colors, textures . . . symmetry."

"You're also impatient," her mother reminded her. "Have a rather short attention span—"

Sara's mouth dropped. "I do not!"

"You've always had trouble sticking to one project, dear. What you call *multitasking* might seem more like a lack of focus to some people."

Sara looked askance. "You don't think it's a good idea to quit my job and become an artist?"

Her mother gave a small, disbelieving laugh. "Being an artist is lonely work, Sara. You'd be working by yourself and wouldn't have much contact with other people. What would you do with all your exuberance? Your public relations skills?"

"That's true." A touch of doubt crept into her voice.

"And what about money? You certainly can't afford to quit your job unless you're ready to move back home. You have a new house, bills to pay—''

Sara cut her a piercing look. ''Okay. You've made your point.''

''However''—her mother pointed her index finger—''your organizational and interpersonal skills will transfer to anything you decide to do.''

''How about cooking?''

''Cooking?'' she repeated, clearly puzzled. ''Why, I don't really know.'' Her mother put her hand to her throat in obvious confusion. ''I've never been much of a cook.''

''Well, neither am I,'' Sara told her. ''I'm all thumbs in a kitchen.''

Her mother settled her hands on her hips. ''I never thought cooking a priority, Sara. I've had other interests, and we were always well off enough to hire a cook.''

''I'm not complaining,'' Sara assured her. ''And I'm not thinking of it as a career.''

Her mother waved a hand dismissively. ''Then take a course. San Francisco has a world-renowned culinary school, and surely there's a French school ... somewhere.'' She frowned. ''What's this sudden interest in cooking?''

Sara shrugged. ''I just thought I might want to learn something new.''

''An excellent idea. You're much too young to be in a rut.'' She pursed her lips thoughtfully. ''Who was the writer who said a rut is nothing more than a shallow grave?'' She fluttered her hand in the air. ''Whoever he was, he was right.'' She narrowed her eyes shrewdly. ''Any other changes you're considering?''

Sara gave her mother an amused look. ''I always thought I'd have children . . . after I find the right man, of course.''

''Children are nothing to joke about,'' her mother scolded. ''You're talking about my grandchildren.''

''Yes, mother.'' Sara smiled sweetly, then turned thoughtful. ''I'm just not sure a career is enough. Or maybe the problem is''—she shrugged—''it's too much.''

Sara scrutinized the two dresses she was considering, but her thoughts centered on Lorenzo. She wished she could talk to him about the firm, but their perspectives were very different. He viewed the firm as a grand prize, but she was beginning to consider her job a stumbling block. The truth was probably somewhere in between. She took a deep breath, forcing her thoughts to the back of her mind. She was worrying when she should be looking forward to a party. ''I've definitely decided on the green.''

Her mother closed her eyes briefly, then smiled in relief. ''Good. We just have time for a quick bite. How about that Italian bistro down on Pier 39?''

''Good idea.'' Sara ran her tongue over her lower lip. ''I'm starved.'' She walked over to a sales clerk.

"Would you please ring this up?" She turned back to her mother. "I met Lorenzo's mother last week."

"Oh?" Her mother's voice took on a curious tone. "How did that come about?"

Sara opened her handbag, rummaged around for her wallet, and retrieved a gold credit card. "Lorenzo invited me out to dinner."

"And brought his mother along?"

Sara gave her a scathing look, then handed the card to the clerk. "Of course not. His mother cooked. We had dinner at her house."

The two women stared at each other for a few seconds, then both smiled.

"Could have knocked me over with a feather, too," Sara commented wryly.

Her mother arched her brows. "So that's where the cooking came from."

"I got a real lesson in not knowing my way around a kitchen," Sara confided. "Maria seems to do everything. She works full time, raised her children by herself, sews clothes for her grandchildren, and cooks like a gourmet." Sara lowered her eyes, then raised them to meet her mother's curious glance. "She even volunteers to teach children to knit."

"Sounds like Wonder Woman to me."

"And—"

"There's more?"

Sara clamped her lips into a thin line. "She's one of the nicest people I've ever met."

''Oh, dear.'' Her mother's hand fluttered to her cheek. ''I might be feeling a little insecure myself.''

Sara caught Lorenzo stealing glances at her as they walked from the parking lot to the brightly lit hall. If she'd needed any reassurance about her new dress or whether sweeping her hair into an old-fashioned French twist had been a good idea, she'd gotten it when she'd answered his knock.

He'd taken a quick breath, then slid his glance downward almost imperceptibly. His eyes had turned dark and mysterious, only what she saw mirrored in his eyes wasn't mysterious at all. It was unmistakably desire.

Startled, she'd swallowed the lump in her throat. It would be too easy to get caught up in the look he'd given her, and she'd already promised herself to keep careful control over her emotions. She'd thought about the situation a lot, and there was only one answer.

Self-control.

She couldn't cross the friendship line. No matter how she felt about him. No matter that he made her heart pound and her palms sweat. No matter that she thought she might be falling in love with him. It was a dilemma with no resolution. Childhood scars, and the ambition and drive resulting from those scars, meant his career would always come first. Those traits were part of his attraction, but they had a downside she'd sworn to avoid.

Lorenzo glanced at her again. "You look beautiful tonight."

The air between them was charged; she smiled widely in an attempt to relieve some of the tension. "Thanks," she teased, though it felt awkward. "You don't look bad yourself."

He wore black slacks with narrow cuffs, a crisp white shirt left open at the collar, and a black leather bomber jacket. If she had to describe the look, it would be a toss between tough-guy chic and drop-dead gorgeous. He'd obviously left his lawyer look at home.

She turned away and allowed herself a secret smile. If the secretaries who'd dubbed him the Harvard Hunk could see him now, he'd be lucky to get out of the office alive.

A smile touched the corners of his mouth as he opened his arms. "New threads. I haven't been in anything besides a three-piece suit all summer."

She took in a big breath and relaxed her shoulders. She almost wished she'd canceled tonight; it would have made everything a lot easier. Easier to ignore the way she felt about him, easier to think she wasn't in for a world of trouble if she didn't watch herself. All she had to do was keep things light. Remember her vow about love and lawyers—that the two didn't mix. Just have a good time. Stop caring so much.

A minute later, they walked through the door and into a large room full of noise, people, and laughter. Lavender and white balloons peppered the ceiling, and crêpe paper streamers curled from the tiered crystal chandelier to the edges of the walls. A four-piece band was setting up to play on a raised stage at the far end of the room. Two rows of round tables lined the perimeter of the room, each draped in white linen and decorated with a vase of lavender carnations.

As they walked through the room, Sara noticed teenage boys wearing boxy black tuxedos standing in small groups. A few were dressed more casually in shirts and slacks or baggy denim pants and vests. Teenage girls swirled by in dresses of brilliant scarlet and candy-apple red, amethyst, electric blue, and varying shades of gold. Sara spotted a few older girls in slinky black, but most looked like they were dressed for a prom.

"Uncle Alejandro! How are you?" Lorenzo shook hands with an attractive, gray-haired man.

"Fine, son, but we missed you at the *Quinceañera* Mass this afternoon. It was very special, celebrating my little girl's coming of age."

Lorenzo opened his hands in apology. "I was working and couldn't get away."

Alejandro nodded, a serious look clouding his expression. "I understand. A man must work." His face brightened as he glanced at Sara. "Who is this beautiful young lady?"

Lorenzo extended his arm. ''Sara Jackson, this is my Uncle Alejandro.''

Alejandro bent his head slightly. ''Thank you for coming to my daughter's *Quinceañera.* It's a special night for her mother and I.''

Just then a little girl, about five or six years old and dressed in a frilly white dress, ran by and almost knocked Sara off her feet.

''Whoa!'' Lorenzo reached out to steady Sara about the same time a boy in a miniature suit and tie dashed by.

Alejandro smiled indulgently and shook his head. ''The courting rituals start younger every year.'' He opened his arms. ''What can you do?''

Sara glanced around the room. ''It's a wonderful party. I'm looking forward to the evening.''

Alejandro dipped his head. ''I'm pleased Lorenzo brought you. As one of the *padrinos,* he is an honored guest. Please . . .'' He gestured grandly. ''Enjoy yourself. I must see to the final preparations.''

As Alejandro walked away, Sara asked, ''What's a *padrino?*''

''A sponsor. *Quinceañeras* are expensive, and the *padrinos* each pay for a little something. Most families have six or seven, sometimes more.'' He scanned the crowded room, nodded at someone and smiled, then turned back to Sara. ''It's the only way some families can afford the expense.''

"Since Laura is both your niece and goddaughter, your families must be close."

"Alejandro isn't really my uncle, so Laura's not my niece."

She glanced at him questioningly.

"His family lived next door when I was a kid. I started calling him uncle because I wanted one. Lucky for me, he didn't object."

Before Sara could think of something to say, he reached down and took her hand. "Come on. Let's get some *horchata*."

"What's that?"

"A sweet rice drink." He squeezed her hand. "I want to say hello to *mamá* and my sisters before the waltz."

Sara felt a wave of apprehension. "Your mother's here? And your sisters?"

"Of course. And my brothers-in-law and their kids." He tugged on her hand. "Come on."

"Waltz?" she whispered under her breath as a feeling of dread washed over her. Suddenly the evening loomed large in front of her, like a tidal wave.

"The waltz is Laura's big moment," Lorenzo explained. "She and her *chambelanes*—escorts," he explained, "have been practicing for weeks."

"And the music afterward? It'll be what kids listen to these days?"

"Sure. But there will be slow numbers, too." He

glanced around the room. "Something for everybody."

Sara's heart sank. Music brought up the issue of dancing, and Sara had two left feet. She couldn't dance.

A half hour later, the drummer played a staccato tapping and the audience all looked toward the stage. Sara and Lorenzo stood watching with his sisters, Consuela and Anna.

Alejandro tapped on the microphone. "My friends, Laura and her *chambelanes* have a very special *Quenceañera* waltz for us. I hope you all enjoy it." The lights dimmed around the edge of the room, leaving the multilayered chandelier glowing in the center of the hall.

Laura walked out of the crowd toward the center of the dance floor. She wore a very full, white lace dress. A short veil of netting fell away from her face, covering her black curls like a cloud. Following behind her were six teenage boys dressed in black tuxedos. The music started and Laura floated, first stiffly, then gracefully, from one *chambelane* to the next. A few minutes later the music rose to a crescendo and she crouched in her hoops for a finale.

The *chambelanes* crowded around her and leaned in, then bent out, one by one. As Laura stood, it was as if she were emerging from a cocoon. The boys bent and lifted her on their shoulders as the guests applauded loudly and cheered.

Lorenzo bent down and cupped his hand next to Sara's ear. "This symbolizes Laura's change from a child into a woman. Now each male *padrino* will dance with her; just a few minutes each because there are so many."

Sara stood with Consuela and Anna while Lorenzo danced with Laura. She liked both sisters, but got on especially well with Anna. She was a few years younger than Sara and expecting her second child. She was also an artist.

Sara was mesmerized by the dancing. "It's so much like a wedding," she said to Consuela.

"Yes. "*Mamá* couldn't afford *Quinceañeras* for us girls, but our daughters will have the celebration. Lorenzo has promised."

Sara glanced back to the dance floor, watching Lorenzo relinquish Laura's hand to Alejandro with a very formal bow. Father and daughter danced for several minutes, then the crowd toasted them with champagne.

Lorenzo walked from the other side of the dance floor toward Sara. When he approached, he bent down close. "Laura did a great job, don't you think?"

She nodded, smiling.

"The *Quinceañera* waltz is very emotional for a father, but also very difficult."

"Why?" she asked.

"It's a public acknowledgment that his little girl is now a woman." Lorenzo glanced down at Sara. "The

Quinceañera is a celebration, but it's also a passage from one part of life into another. Laura is also acknowledging responsibility for herself. It's a statement of separation from her parents.''

"Fifteen is a little young for that."

Lorenzo glanced back out at the dance floor where Laura stood, surrounded by friends. "Perhaps, but not so long ago Laura would already be married and having babies."

"Times change," Sara countered with a laugh. "She's got her whole life for marriage and children."

Lorenzo nodded. "And I hope she takes her time. When I was fifteen I wondered if I'd live to be thirty, let alone have a family."

Sara opened her mouth, but clamped it shut without saying anything. *Keep it light,* she reminded herself. *Nothing too personal. It's enough that you're getting to know his mother and sisters. Watch out or the next thing you know, you'll be babysitting!* Oddly enough, that didn't sound like such a bad idea.

The musicians started playing a hot new *cumbia* tune, and Lorenzo swayed slightly back and forth to the music. He hadn't been to a party in years. Law school and work had kept him too busy to think about having fun. He reached down and took Sara's hand.

She glanced up at him.

"Come on." He grinned. "Let's dance. I'll teach you the *banda*."

"*Banda?*"

He tugged on her hand. "Come on. It'll be fun."

The blood drained from her face and she shook her head. "No. Really, I can't dance."

"Sure you can," he insisted with a wicked grin. "If you can move your hips, you can do the *banda*."

"But that's just it," she said softly under her breath. "I can't."

Chapter Nine

Lorenzo pulled harder until Sara had no choice but to follow along behind him. He led her to the center of the dance floor, directly under the tiered chandelier that cast a golden glow over the dancers. He stood looking down at her. She was the most beautiful woman he'd ever seen. He liked the way she'd twisted her hair up in the back, leaving a few wispy curls around her face. She looked soft and sweet, just like an angel.

He reached out and took her hands, then placed them a few inches below his own waist. He leaned down, speaking loudly so she could hear. "It will help you feel which way I'm going to move."

She nodded.

He gently placed his hands on each side of her

waist. As he swiveled his hips to the music, he moved her body with his. When he took a step backward and pulled her toward him, she stumbled, but managed to catch herself. Glancing up, she grinned self-consciously.

"Sorry!" she yelled over the blare of trumpets and the staccato of drums.

He shook his head and shrugged to indicate he couldn't hear what she was saying.

She moved awkwardly at first, but within a few minutes was moving right with him. The occasional jolt of her hip against his thigh sent a shiver through him until finally he reached out, took her hand, and swung her into the circle of his arms. She settled against his chest with a soft thud and he held her there.

He looked at her with frank enjoyment. Her breathing was labored from dancing, her emerald eyes full of excitement. A rush of pink stained her cheeks as she gave him a brilliant smile.

"And you said you couldn't dance," he teased.

She laughed. "I can't. You just know how to make a girl look good."

The lights dimmed and the band started up again. This time the beat was slow, the melody soft. "One more?" he asked, still gazing into her eyes.

She nodded.

He took her hand, laid it against his chest, and covered it with his. Then he confidently encircled her in his other arm and moved to the music. She buried her face against his chest, her head fitting snugly under his chin. He could feel the silky strands of her hair, smell her perfume. It was sweet and flowery, reminding him of a summer's day. The sensations disturbed his concentration, and he swallowed hard.

She stumbled against him a couple of times, but he kept her steady. Kept his arms around her. Kept moving slowly to the flow of the music until he felt her relax enough to follow him smoothly and expertly. He led her into a few turns, and she stayed with him.

He was surprised at how easily she fit in his arms— and his life. It suddenly hit him that was exactly where she belonged. With him. He leaned back and looked at her. It was if it were the first time he was really seeing her. And what he saw scared him. Just as quickly, he cradled her in his arms.

''What's wrong?'' she asked softly, her mouth against his chest.

He remained silent and closed his eyes briefly as feelings of love engulfed him. It was a fierce feeling that consumed every other thought. He realized this was where they'd been headed all this time. Their working together, becoming friends, the times he'd turned away from her because he was afraid of how she made him feel. Vulnerable. Strong. Happy.

Sara had been there when he needed her. She'd cared. And he realized that all along he'd been falling in love with her. She was the one woman, the only woman, who could make him happy.

He stopped and moved slightly away from her.

"What is it?" she asked again.

He took a deep breath and steeled himself. He knew what he had to do. He had no other choice. "Let's go outside."

She grinned. "Had enough of dancing lessons?"

He didn't answer, just took her by the hand, and they threaded their way among the dancers and through the glass doors leading to a long patio stretching the length of the building.

"Oh, look!" Sara glanced up at the moon, a thick yellow globe against a blue-black sky. "A full moon."

Lorenzo pulled her into his embrace. "A lover's moon," he said hoarsely.

She looked startled, her mouth slightly open as if she were going to speak, only she didn't. She just fluttered her lashes, a look of uncertainty settling over her features.

He took one hand and gently ran it through her hair, then around the arc of her face. "You're so beautiful." He bent down and brushed a gentle kiss against her forehead, then each cheek.

She closed her eyes briefly, then opened them. He saw the question in her eyes.

"What are you thinking?" he asked.

She didn't answer, just slowly shook her head.

He whispered her name, then gently pressed his lips to hers, caressing her mouth more than kissing. When he felt her relax and begin to respond, his thoughts spun. He deepened the kiss, although his brain registered the order to stop. He didn't want to stop. For a few sweet seconds, his heart and mind were filled with her. Her smell, her touch. Then he forced himself to pull away. He didn't want to overwhelm or frighten her.

He dropped his hands and stepped back a pace. He took a deep breath, his feelings a trip-hammer in his chest. He turned sideways and jammed his hands in his pockets as he tried to figure out what to do. He'd never felt so close to anyone, never cared so much. He realized with a start that Sara was all that mattered.

"Lorenzo, what is it?"

He slowly turned around and looked at her.

"Lorenzo?"

He slowly shook his head, then opened his arms. "I guess there's only one way to do this."

"Do what?"

He swallowed hard, reached out, and took her hands. "Tell you I'm in love with you."

The color drained from her face. It was as if her thoughts came together all at once. She was swimming through a haze of feelings and desires, but the one that swept over her like a tidal wave was the almost overwhelming desire to run away. She took in a short breath and managed to repeat the word that scared her the most. "Love?"

Although he nodded, his eyes mirrored his disbelief. "I'm kind of in shock myself. But I think it's been there all the time. Just waiting for us to recognize what was really happening."

She bit down on her bottom lip. "I don't know if I can do this, Lorenzo."

"Do what? Love me?"

The bottom fell out of her stomach. It was as if she were rushing toward a precipice and deciding whether to jump. She felt as if her breath were cut off. She put one hand up to her throat, trying to lessen her sense of being hemmed in. "Oh, Lorenzo. I do love you."

The look he gave her sent her pulse spinning, but she knew she had no choice but to go on—to finish what she had to say. She shook her head sadly. "We have to be honest, Lorenzo. It would never work."

Lines creased his brow. "Why not?"

She turned away and stared out into the darkness. The stars reminded her of the long row of lights strung between the girders of the Golden Gate Bridge. It was a long, dangerous rope she couldn't, or wouldn't, climb. "I've been doing a lot of thinking the past couple of weeks," she said, then turned back around, hugging her arms. "I think that's in large part because of you." She paused a moment, collecting her thoughts. "There's something we need to talk about."

"What's that?"

"My ex-husband."

Blood siphoned from his face. "Do you still love him?"

"No." She shook her head. "Of course not."

He relaxed a little, then shrugged. "Then there's nothing to talk about. Dwelling on the past gets in the way of the future." He opened his arms. "If I'd done that, where would I be now?"

"I'm afraid that's part of the problem. Where you are now."

"That's a problem?" he asked, dumbfounded.

"You're a strong man, Lorenzo. I think your strength may sometimes blind you to what's truly important."

"What do you mean?"

She shook her head. "My ex-husband was the same. Ambitious. Driven. He was more married to his career than to me."

Lorenzo stared at her but said nothing.

"I care about you, Lorenzo, but I don't want that kind of life. I want a family, children. A man who'll spend weekends doing things with me." She lifted one hand casually. "Picnics, working around the house together, going to the park . . ."

"I don't get it." A sudden chill hung on the edge of his words. "I want those things, too. But are you asking me to give up the law, knowing how many years I've worked to get where I am? And how much I want this?''

She shook her head, then let out a long breath. ''No. No, of course not.''

He bridged the space between them and clasped her hands. ''All I know is that I love you.'' His voice challenged, but his eyes had darkened with emotion. ''But I also love my work. It's what a man does, Sara. I have to provide a home, a good life for my family.'' He shook his head. ''I can't change that. It's part of who I am.''

''I don't want to come second,'' she insisted, pulling away and taking a step backward. ''I want more than that.''

''We can have it all, Sara. ''Just give me some time. You know I can't do it in forty hours a week. Not now. In a few years, things will be different. Can't you see that?''

His eyes told her he believed what he was saying. Her heart knew they didn't stand a chance. Even if he wanted to slow down, joining a large firm meant joining the rat race for the long haul. But could she give him up? She was torn between love and fear and didn't know which way to turn. If she let herself go for one moment, she knew she'd do whatever he asked. She loved him that much. But would she lose herself in the process?

''I don't know, Lorenzo,'' she said, pressing the

back of her hand to her lips to hide their trembling. "You'll have to give me some time."

Lorenzo sat at the kitchen table, watching his mother and trying not to yawn. He'd taken Sara home early last night, then spent the night slipping from one dream to the next, always searching for something that remained just outside his grasp.

His mother stood at the stove, one hand resting on her hip, the other stirring a steaming pot of soup. It was a memory Lorenzo had carried with him for as long as he could remember. *Mamá* cooking the evening meal, making casseroles and chocolate chip cookies for neighbors too embarrassed to ask for help at the end of the month. She was always taking care of people. Pretty soon, the tables would be turned and he'd be taking care of her.

"Are you sure I can't help?" he asked.

Maria shook her head. "It's almost ready." She glanced over at him. "I enjoy cooking; you know that."

"*Mamá,* you work too hard."

She waved one hand dismissively. "All right. You can toss the salad. It's in the refrigerator."

As he walked behind her to reach the refrigerator, he inhaled deeply and smacked his lips. "Nobody makes *sopa albóndigas* like you, *mamá.*

She gave him a quick, uncertain look. "I hope the meatballs aren't too spicy." She turned back to the stove. "We have tamales, too. Are you sure that's enough for lunch?"

He ran one hand over his stomach. "Unless you want me to get fat." He set the salad on the table, then rummaged in a drawer until he found two large serving spoons.

Maria watched him carefully, checking to see that everything stayed in the bowl as he tossed the salad. Satisfied, she picked up two bright yellow pot holders, opened the door to the stove, and took out a casserole. She carefully carried the pan over to the table and placed it on a wrought-iron trivet. Then she went back to the stove and ladled soup into two earthenware bowls.

Carrying the blue-rimmed bowls to the table, she gave Lorenzo a shrewd look. "There's enough for at least one more. I should have invited Sara."

Lorenzo met her gaze, then glanced away. He piled a mound of salad on his plate, then served his mother.

Maria glanced at him out of the corner of her eye. "She has a healthy appetite . . . your Sara."

Lorenzo sighed. He recognized that voice. The sweet one his mother used when she wanted something. Well, that was what he'd been planning to do— tell her about Sara. He might as well get on with it.

"Sit down, *mamá.* I have something to tell you."

Maria paled. "Is this bad news?"

"No. No." He shook his head. "It's just . . . complicated."

Maria slipped into the chair opposite him and folded her hands in her lap.

Lorenzo ran a hand across his forehead, then through his hair. "*Mamá . . .*" He paused, took a sip of water, then leaned his elbows on the table, linking his fingers together. "I'm in love with Sara."

Maria's mouth dropped slightly.

"I'm going to ask her to marry me"—Lorenzo paused for a second, then finished in a rush—"and I'd like your blessing."

Maria looked down slightly, hiding her expression. She needed time to think.

He flung both hands open and let out a huge breath. "There. It's done." He pushed his chair back and stood, shoving his hands in his pockets.

"Sara seems like a nice girl." She slowly unfolded her napkin and placed it on her lap. "But are you sure this is love?"

He didn't miss a heartbeat. "Absolutely."

"But you hardly know each other." She kept her hands clasped to mask her apprehension. "How long has it been? A month?"

"A little more," he mumbled, then shook his head vigorously. "I know it sounds crazy, *mamá*—"

"Loving someone is not crazy," she broke in reassuringly. "But Sara is from a different world. How can she know who you are? Or where you come from?"

He paced a few feet away, then turned back. When

he did, he stood tall, feet braced apart. His eyes shone with determination. He knew what he wanted. He wanted Sara. But almost as importantly, he wanted his mother's approval. Without it, there would be a big hole in his life, and his heart. His mother was strong willed, and they'd had their differences in the past. But if she intended to fight him on this, she was in for a big surprise. He intended to wage a war.

"I understand your concerns," he said, his voice strong and resolute. "But whatever differences Sara and I have aren't that important."

"Of course they are!" Maria insisted with a deep frown. "And who will take care of you? She doesn't even know how to cook!"

"I'm a grown man. I don't need someone to take care of me, and that's not why I want to marry Sara." He got up and started pacing, running a hand along the back of his neck, an angry frown darkening his features. "I love her. That's all that matters. Everything else is just . . . details we'll have to work out. Sara and I are a lot alike, *mamá*. We care about the same things."

"Her career?"

He frowned darkly. "Yes, I care about her career. Her drive and energy are part of why I love her. I know you think I should have a wife who wants to stay home, but it's what I want"—he jabbed his chest with his thumb—"that's important."

Maria ran her hand along his cheek, thinking about

her son and how fiercely she loved him. "You were always a difficult child," she said with a sigh. "Headstrong, willful."

He smiled. "Like you, *mamá.*"

She returned his smile, but it was hesitant. "If it's what you want."

Lorenzo took her hand and brought it to his lips. "Sara and I will have beautiful children."

Maria raised her chin slightly. "And intelligent."

"Then we have your blessing?"

She nodded and closed her eyes briefly.

A look of relief brightened his face, then his brow furrowed. "There's only one problem." He came to his feet, took a few steps, and leaned against the wall, crossing his arms.

"What is this problem?"

"I told Sara last night that I love her." He pursed his lips. "But things didn't go well." He gave Maria a doubtful look. "I'm not sure how she feels."

Maria raised her head in shock, then she narrowed her eyes. "Of course she loves you. What woman would not?"

Lorenzo smiled, tipping his head. "I'm not an easy man to love."

"Of course you are." Maria wagged her finger. "You must work this problem out. If you love her, you will do it."

He bent and kissed her cheek. "Thank you,

mamá.'' He sat and let out a long breath. ''Let's finish lunch. Suddenly I'm starved.''

Maria gave him a guarded look, then allowed herself a secret smile. She accepted that he was in love. Why else would he be so uncertain? So worried about whatever this *problem* was. Surely it was a little spat, a lover's quarrel. She would find a way to help. And the best way to do that was to talk to Sara.

She would call her and invite her to lunch next week. Better yet, she would offer to teach Sara how to cook some of Lorenzo's favorite meals. What better way to get to know her future daughter-in-law?

Chapter Ten

Lorenzo tried his best to forget about Sara for the entire week. He called her once but kept the conversation brief. He had to focus on the most important week in his life.

He spent three days cramming for the bar exam and another three taking the five-part written examination. He spent evenings poring over textbooks and interpreting case law before remembering to eat something, then crawling exhausted into bed.

His entire career hinged on whether he passed the bar. Last year, sixty-three percent had made the grade. Some of the best students failed on their first try, and the top-notch firms didn't hire them. And all his offers of employment were contingent on passing. Just because you survived three years of law school didn't mean you got to practice law; it just meant you had a ticket to try.

Now it was over. He'd know in a few days if he'd passed. Not that he had any doubts, but that piece of paper meant everything.

He had another dilemma. His last day at the immigration clinic, Bud Wagner had offered him a job. What with the on-campus interviews at Harvard, and clerking the last two summers, he had a total of five job offers.

Now he had to choose. But, first, he had to decide what he wanted to do with the rest of his life.

Sara glanced at her watch again, then continued down the thickly carpeted hallway toward Mac's office. He'd asked her to be there at five o'clock and she was ten minutes late. Not a good beginning.

The door to his office was open; she glanced inside. Mac was seated behind his desk, reading from an open book. He held a small microphone in his right hand. She rapped her knuckles against the door three times. He laid the microphone on the desk and leaned back heavily in his high-backed chair. "Come in."

"My meeting with Pat Clayton went later than I expected," she apologized, taking one of the chairs positioned in front of his desk. She crossed her legs and adjusted the skirt of her tawny gold linen suit.

"The next recruiting meeting's scheduled for"—

he glanced at his calendar, then at Sara—"day after tomorrow?"

Sara nodded.

Mac sat back in his chair, giving her a speculative look. "Which clerks get your vote this year?"

"My first round is Ken Thornton, Anne Lockwood, and Bob Simms. But almost all—"

"What about Kramer?" he interrupted.

She took a deep breath. "King's work is excellent, but his judgment is lacking. Of course, he's young. It's a call either way."

Mac's eyes narrowed slightly. "Do you have an answer from Duran?"

She took a deep breath and returned his gaze calmly. "No, not yet."

"Have you talked to him?"

"Not the past week. He was taking the bar exam."

Matt looked at her, lips pursed in disapproval. "Did you call to wish him luck? Any contact at all?"

Sara didn't want to lie; of course she'd talked to Lorenzo. But she'd never brought up his offer from the firm, or asked whether he intended to accept. "I didn't press him for an answer."

Mac's nostrils flared briefly, and from the impatient look he gave her, Sara knew he was angry. His frown grew darker by the second.

She arched her brows. "If he wants the extra five thousand signing bonus, he's only got another week."

"That's not the point." Mac leaned forward slightly. "I asked you—"

"I know what you asked," she interrupted. "And I've given it a lot of thought." She took in a deep breath and opened both hands. "The fact is, I've decided to leave the firm."

Mac's frown deepened. "What brought this on? Surely not Duran."

"No. It's not this. It's a lot of things." She thought for a minute, struggling between the need to keep silent and the need to tell him how she felt. "Mac, you hired me for a job no one believed in and challenged me to change everyone's mind about recruiting. The last couple of years have been important for me."

"And the firm," he added quietly. "You've been an asset, Sara."

She nodded slightly. "Thank you. But life keeps moving on. It just slides by whether you make a conscious decision to do what you want or let circumstances decide things for you. I've taken my job as far as it can go; any longer and it becomes a rut." She bit down on her lip, hoping she hadn't offended him. "Ruts are comfortable, of course, but they keep you in one place and I've been there long enough."

Mac appeared to struggle for a moment, then shrugged with resignation. "It sounds like your mind's made up. I won't try and change it." He pushed back his chair and stood. "We'll need to find a replacement as soon as possible."

Sara rose quickly, knowing she was being dismissed. If Mac was anything, he was consistent. "I may know someone," she said, turning to leave. "He's qualified, and his firm is downsizing."

She looked back over her shoulder. "It would be a good match. I'll call him if you like."

"Your recommendation means a lot, Sara. Get me his résumé as soon as possible."

She stopped a moment, pursing her lips. "I've enjoyed working for you, Mac. You've been a great teacher."

"And you've turned the job into something quite remarkable." He walked over and offered his hand.

She shook it briefly. "Thank you."

He nodded once, then turned back to his desk.

Sara walked through the doorway and down the hall. She glanced at the original lithographs and paintings decorating the walls, the heavy tapestry curtains framing spectacular views of the city, the plush carpeting, and the expensive furniture. Even after three years, Davis & MacGregor still impressed her. Then she thought of all the law students who'd walked through these same hallways, researching cases and writing briefs until all hours of the night. They'd all been impressed—with their surroundings, the caliber of people, and the high-profile cases.

She had reached a turning point, leaving one part

of her life to begin another. There was only one problem—she wasn't sure which direction to head. And it looked like she'd be traveling alone. The evening hadn't gone well, and neither had mentioned when they'd see each other again.

Lorenzo hadn't called. He'd apparently chosen his career over her. She tried to tell herself it was just as well she found out now, before he broke her heart, but she had a hard time believing it was over. Somehow, she'd forget him and forge a path of her own— spending her time working at something that gave meaning to her life. She thought about cleaning out her office, but changed her mind. She wouldn't be leaving until her replacement was on board. Instead, she took a searing glance at her in-box, grabbed her purse, and headed home.

The temperature was still almost eighty when she got home, so she changed into shorts and a bright pink T-shirt she'd bought in Cancún. She scrambled two eggs, threw in some cheese, and popped a slice of sourdough bread in the toaster. She took her dinner, along with a pencil and paper, out to the patio off the kitchen.

She wanted to get a start on renovating the downstairs, but didn't know what she wanted to do with the huge el-shaped space. It was much too large for just a sitting and dining area. There was enough room for just about anything she wanted to do; she just had to figure out what that was.

Deep in thought, she frowned when she heard the doorbell. By the time she walked inside and got to the door, the bell chimed again.

"I'm coming," she muttered, opening the door.

Lorenzo stood framed in the doorway—thumbs hooked in the belt loops of faded jeans, a pale blue shirt molding his chest, thick black hair all wind-blown. His shadowy dark eyes didn't look at her, but saw right into her soul.

She gulped, and her heart sank to the pit of her stomach. Her plans retreated as quickly as the out-going ocean tide. How could she think he was out of her life? That she could just go on living without him? She opened her mouth to speak, but no words came out.

He took a step forward, then stopped. "We need to talk. Can I come in?"

The look he gave her made it impossible to say no, but her pride made her object. She straightened her shoulders and thrust her chin forward. "I told you how I feel. I'm not suggesting you have to agree with me." The first licks of pain glinted in her eyes. "I know you have your life to live, too." The last words came out in one long breath, and when she was fin-ished, she sucked in air, desperate to feel oxygen in her lungs.

"I'm sorry I haven't called, Sara, but I've been working."

She closed her eyes as a sinking feeling engulfed

her. Then she opened them and slowly shook her head. "Yes, I know. Your work comes first."

"Are you going to invite me in?" This time his voice sounded like a barely contained growl.

She grimaced and swung the door open. Might as well get it over with, she told herself, not looking forward to the prospect.

He stepped in and closed the door firmly behind him.

"Sit down." She motioned toward the sofa, the only piece of furniture in the huge room.

He blew out a heavy sigh and plowed both hands through his disheveled hair. "I don't think I can. I've got too much to say."

A warning voice whispered in her head. "The bar exam—you passed, didn't you?"

"Yes, yes," he answered quickly, then reached out and hugged her to him and just as quickly let her go again.

"What is it?" she gasped.

"It's everything!" he shouted. "You . . . me." He waved both hands in the air. "You sit down. I have to pace."

She sat on the edge of the sofa, looking up at him, waiting.

"I've got what I want, Sara. Well . . . almost everything." He shook his head. "I sent letters to all the firms that offered me jobs."

"Which one did you accept?"

"None. I'm going out on my own. I'm opening a private practice."

"What?" She gasped. "How?"

"Well, I don't actually have an office yet. That's one of the details I haven't worked out yet." He glanced at her, his eyes blazing. "I've been hired as corporate counsel for Harper & Ross."

The blood siphoned from her face. "The advertising firm? Don't they do the Nike ads on TV?"

"Among others," he confirmed proudly.

"But how?" Suddenly she snapped her fingers and jumped up. "Jack Tarkington! You know him."

Lorenzo nodded. "I did some legal work for one of his employees. Things worked out pretty well, and he's retained me to do his personal work, too." He paced a few feet past the sofa, then back again. "The immigration clinic is backlogged and wants me to handle some overflow work. And Aaron Brooks wants me to take on a few minor cases." He glanced at her, worry etched across his features. "How do you think Mac would feel about that?"

"I'm not sure," she answered honestly. "But Aaron told Mac he wanted you to work for him." She narrowed her eyes. "Did you call Aaron or did he—"

"He invited me to a dinner party and I called to decline. I couldn't take time out from studying. One thing led to another."

He shrugged.

"Then I don't see how Mac can complain. Not that he'll be happy about it." Her brow furrowed. "But business is business. He knows the game."

They looked at each other for a moment, then Sara broke into a big grin. "I can't believe it. I didn't know you'd even thought about going into private practice."

He closed the distance between them, then folded her into his arms. "I hadn't. Not until you gave me an ultimatum."

"I didn't give you an—"

"Yes you did." He reached up and touched her nose with his index finger, then gave her a smile that lit her heart like a blast of sunshine. Suddenly she knew everything would be all right. He was in her life. He'd had a choice and he'd come back. She reached her hands around his neck and buried her face against his chest. "I love you so much," she whispered breathlessly.

"I love you, too." Lorenzo eased back and looked at her, then ran his hand through her hair, letting the strands fall like silk through his fingers. "I thought a lot about what you said, Sara. How you feel about things; what you need to make you happy. And the more I thought about it, I realized the answer was simple."

"It was?"

He nodded. "I just had to figure out what it takes to make *me* happy, and the answer was right there in front of me all the time. You make me happy, Sara. The answer is you.'' His eyes still locked on hers, he lowered his head and brushed his lips against hers.

Without conscious thought, she kissed him back, surrendering to wonderful currents of sensation for a brief, fleeting moment. All too soon, she felt him pull away.

''Will you marry me, Sara?''

Her mouth dropped. ''Marry—''

''Yes. Marry me.''

''Don't you think it's a little too soon?''

''No. And I don't want a long engagement. How about September?''

She gasped, unwound her arms from around his neck, and swatted at him playfully. ''That's a month away! Besides, I have a lot of decisions to make myself.''

''What could be more important than choosing a wedding date?'' he reasoned.

''Figuring out what I'm going to do for a living, that's what. I'm quitting Davis & MacGregor.''

His quick intake of breath was audible. ''Why?''

She pursed her lips and opened her hands. ''I wouldn't tell *you* to get a life if I wasn't willing to get one of my own. I'm going to find a job working fewer hours and pare my expenses down as much as possible.''

He laced his fingers around hers, listening intently.

"I thought maybe I could manage a small office or even do secretarial work if I have to."

"So you'll have a lot of free time to . . ." His voice trailed off in a question.

"That's the scary part," she admitted. "I've accepted a commission for two Native American baskets from the Dodd gallery. That's a start."

He leaned over and kissed her. "That's wonderful. Congratulations."

She kissed him back, then let her gaze scan the large, empty room. "And I want to figure out what to do with this place." Suddenly she grinned, sucked in her lower lip, and glanced up at him, a purposeful gleam in her eye. She put one hand on her hip and started slowly walking around the room.

"What are you doing?

She pursed her lips in a tight line. "You're going into business for yourself, right?"

He nodded.

"And you'll need office space."

"Yes, of course—"

"And someone to set up your practice, handle the books." His brow furrowed.

"Furnish the office, hire a receptionist . . ." She let her words dangle off into the air, then smiled.

He folded his arms and gave her a stony look. "Are you suggesting you be my landlord?"

She walked over and placed her hands on his shoulders, then ran them along his arms, finally covering his hands and forcing them to his sides. She stood on tiptoes and kissed him square on the mouth.

"I'm suggesting a partnership."

His frown deepened. "Business partners?"

She grinned. "Correct me if I'm wrong, Mr. Duran, but I thought I heard a marriage proposal."

He broke away from her and gave her an exasperated look. "I did, but now you're talking . . . business. What are you getting at, Sara?"

She felt all the worry fall away from her. It was as if someone had turned on a switch and she saw her future—*their* future. She reached out and took his hand. "I'm talking about a partnership, Lorenzo. One that fills our life from morning to night. Partnership in life. Partnership in love."

He closed his eyes and threw his head back. Then a smile spread across his face and he reached out and grabbed her, swinging her around until she squealed. "You said yes!" He set her back down. "You did say yes, didn't you?"

Her face was flushed, her eyes bright with laughter. She nodded enthusiastically. "It's a package deal."

His face turned serious. "Only on one condition," he said, kissing her soundly on the mouth. "I have some money saved; that, my client base, and a good business plan will get me a start-up loan. We use that to renovate the downstairs into offices and a studio for you."

Her mouth gaped as she realized what he was suggesting. Her gaze flitted around the room. "The downstairs alone is over a thousand square feet. There would be plenty of room for"—she bit down on her lower lip and clasped her hands together—"us to work together!"

A grin spread over his face, his eyes blazing with enthusiasm. "Do we have a deal? Partners in marriage *and* work?"

Sara arched one brow, then stood on her tiptoes and kissed him so hard he almost fell backwards. "It's a dream come true," she shouted happily. "We'll be together every day."

He took her hands and pulled her close.

As Sara's arms settled around his waist, Lorenzo looked deep into her eyes and felt a peace settle over him. "I never thought I'd find you, Sara," he whispered. "I've spent my life feeling like there was something . . . missing."

She tried to kiss him, but he stopped her.

"No, let me finish. I want to tell you how I feel."

"Then can we kiss?"

He smiled. "Yes, then we can kiss." He hugged her tight, then nuzzled her ear. "You're what's been missing in my life. And now that I've found you, my very beautiful, and very perfect partner, I'm never going to let you go."

"Is that a promise?" she whispered against his neck.

"Yes—a promise for always."